CAN'T YOU JUST GET OVER IT?

Catherine Blackmore

First published 2019
by Rowanvale Books Ltd
The Gate
Keppoch Street
Roath
Cardiff
CF24 3JW
www.rowanvalebooks.com

A CIP catalogue record for this book is available from the British Library.
ISBN: 978-1-912655-14-4

ACKNOWLEDGEMENTS

Thank you to my parents for having faith in me.

To my husband, for the love and support. There were times, while writing this book, I needed it. Love you.

Karen, thank you for all the help while I wrote the book.

Nina, thank you for your advice on the book.

To the girls, who put a smile on my face and always checked up on me. Love you.

Thank you to Rowanvale Books for all your advice and help putting this book together.

CHAPTER 1

I could see houses in the distance, and a sense of relief swept over me. If I reached them, I would be safe. I was running as fast as I could, but I didn't seem to be getting anywhere. Then I remembered why I was running and looked behind me.

There was a man with a knife. In the dark, I couldn't see his face. Suddenly the terror was back, sweat pouring down my face. Tired, I wanted to stop running, but I couldn't. I couldn't even remember how I got here.

I turned around. He was gaining on me. But how? He was only walking, in no rush. *Someone help me.*

Suddenly, my head screamed with pain and I staggered backwards. I looked up; a lamppost was in front of me. I must have run into it.

I felt lightheaded and I needed to stop. I needed to lie down, but the man would catch up if I did.

I looked around at my surroundings again and things still looked familiar to me… *Oh God no— please tell me I haven't been running in circles or, worse, on the spot.*

Breath tickled the back of my neck. I slowly turned around. He was right behind me. I quickly backed away, but he kept with my pace. Something solid slammed into my back. I glanced—a wall. No escape now.

The shiny silver blade cut through the darkness above my head. I screamed in the hope that someone would hear me. My heart raced, my whole body was shaking, and the knife quickly and swiftly came down towards my chest.

I was still screaming when I opened my eyes to find myself sitting up in my bed. There was no blood, no pain. Was it a nightmare? It must have been, but it felt so real.

I quickly got out of bed and headed to the bathroom. I put the light on and looked in the mirror at the image staring back at me. My brown hair was all over the place; the sweat was still pouring down my face and my hazel eyes were wide with terror. My shirt was covered in sweat, so I took it off but, before I put a fresh one on, I cleaned my face to get rid of the sweat. I dried myself and headed back to my bedroom. Still shaking, I switched the lights on. I grabbed my mobile phone and started to dial my boyfriend Mason's number. When I looked at the time and saw it was two-thirty in the morning, I ended the call. There was no point in us both being awake because of the nightmare. Even if this was the second time that I'd had it that week.

My bed was damp because I'd been sweating so much, but I curled up to sleep on the other side of the bed, deciding to change the bedding in the morning.

When the alarm went off at six o'clock, to say I'd had no sleep was an understatement. I got into the shower hoping that it would wake me up. I headed downstairs to make myself breakfast. None of the cereals appealed to me, so I opted for toast instead. After I buttered my toast, I put the bread on top of the toaster. Sitting down to eat at the small table in the kitchen, I lit up a cigarette. Without warning, panic set in. Terror crept over me like in the dream. What if it hadn't just been a bad dream? What if the nightmare was real?

The smell of plastic hit me. I quickly looked around my kitchen and realised that I'd put the plastic wrapper the bread was in on the toaster and—stupid me—switched the toaster back on. The smell went through me. I hastily removed the bread from the toaster and switched it off. How could I have been so clumsy? I definitely needed more sleep.

As I headed out the door, Mason pulled up. His silver car had seen better days, but for some reason, he refused to part with it. He asked if I wanted a lift to work.

I couldn't help but smile when I saw him, especially after what had happened last night. I got into his car and gave him a kiss on the cheek. His green eyes smiled before he pulled away. He was dressed in a suit for work and his wavy black hair had been swept back, which never suited him. If he would just brush it and let it fall naturally, it would suit him better.

We had been dating for a year and my friends were saying that we should be engaged, but to be honest, I was in no rush. I was enjoying what we had and, as the saying goes, I didn't want to rock the boat.

I lit a cigarette, winding down the window.

"What are you doing this Saturday?" Mason asked.

I looked at him. "Why—what do you have in mind?"

"I will ignore that you can't give a straight answer, but a friend from work is having a party and thought you might want to go."

"I'll think about it."

As he pulled up outside my work, Mason leaned over and said, "Emily, please come to the party. It will be fun—I promise."

I should have told him what had happened last night, but he'd have thought I was crazy. To be honest, the way I was feeling, I really didn't want to go to this party on Saturday, but I put my feelings aside. "Alright, I will go. See you later?"

Mason kissed me. "I'll be over at eight o'clock."

I watched him pull away and then made my way to the back of the building to 'the fag shed', so I could have a cigarette before work. On my way back to the building, I noticed a figure out of the corner of my eye. When I turned to look, there was someone in the distance, dressed in black, just standing there with no expression. Was that a knife they were holding? Fear made me want to scream but stole the sound from my mouth.

I tore my eyes away and ran for the building.

CHAPTER 2

Work was finally over. I opened the door and relief washed over me. My colleagues had been concerned about me, but I'd refused to go home. Some had thought I'd run to work because of the state I was in. I made up an excuse and told them I hadn't had much sleep due to not feeling well. The sleep part was true, so it wasn't a total lie.

I went straight to my kitchen, putting the kettle on because machine tea is nothing like the real thing. The experience this morning had put me on edge, and when the phone rang, I jumped and knocked my cup of tea over. My heart raced as I answered the phone.

"Hello," I said nervously.

"Em, I tried ringing your mobile but you didn't answer." Mason didn't sound happy, but at this point, I didn't care.

"It must be on silent…" I trailed off before my emotions got the better of me.

"Are you OK? You sound off."

Mason knew me well enough to know something was wrong. I ignored the question and asked, "Are you coming over?"

"I finished early, so thought I'd come straight over. I just called to let you know."

Happy to hear that, I placed the phone back in its cradle. I cleaned up the tea I had spilled and made a fresh cup. Before long, Mason knocked on my door. When I opened it, he said, "You look terrible."

As he shut the door, I swung my arms around

him. He embraced me and said softly, "Tell me what's wrong."

In his green eyes, I saw the concern he had for me. I held his hand and walked into the living room.

We sat down and I explained everything that had happened over the last few days. He thought for a moment.

"Maybe you're just stressed."

Had I heard him right? His answer to the nightmares and what I'd seen today at work was just down to stress—that was it. I exploded. "Stress? That's your answer? I knew I shouldn't have said anything to you! Do you know what? You can leave."

Mason just sat there looking shocked. His husky voice replied calmly, "I just gave a suggestion. What do you think it is then?"

I glared at him. "How the hell would I know? But if I thought it was stress then I'd be agreeing with you! Now leave."

Mason stood up from the sofa. He seemed taller when I didn't have my heels on. He firmly said, "I'm not leaving, because this is always your way. I say something you don't like, and you always ask me to leave. Well, I'm saying no this time."

"Fine. But you can sleep on the sofa."

As I turned to leave, he shouted after me, "That's fine with me!"

Having dinner in silence was horrible, but neither of us would back down, all because he'd said it could be stress. The more I thought about it, was it possible? Once it was ten o'clock, I went to my bedroom. Mason followed me.

I turned to look at him and said in an even tone, "Here is the blanket and pillow." I forced them into his hands.

"You can't be serious?" he said with shock.

I didn't reply, just pushed him out the door and shut it behind him.

As he walked down the stairs, I heard him say, "This is fucking stupid." He was right, but I wasn't going to back down. I was still mad. I was lying there, debating whether or not to go and apologise, when I finally closed my eyes.

My bedroom door swung open and suddenly I was awake. At first, I thought it was Mason coming to bed, but that figure was in the doorway, the one from work. He had a knife. Screaming for help, I scrambled out of bed and rushed towards my bedroom window. How had this person got into my house? Was Mason OK? Or had he killed him?

The darkness hid the man's face. I tried to turn on the lamp. It wouldn't work. The man walked towards me, knife in hand. I turned to look out of the window. There were people below. I tried to open the window, but it was stuck, so I banged on it as I screamed to get someone's attention. No one heard my cries for help.

I turned back. The man was in front of me, holding my arm. Terrified, I still screamed. With one hand, he shook me vigorously, and the other raised the knife.

"Emily, wake up!"

When I opened my eyes, Mason was over me, shaking me and saying, "I thought you'd never wake up."

I finally broke down in tears. He sat next to me and held me without saying another word.

CHAPTER 3

"You can't go to work," Mason said as I got dressed.

"I'll be OK, I promise." I didn't really feel that way, but I didn't want to let on to Mason.

He raised his voice and stated, "From what I saw last night, I don't think you are. Maybe you need to see the doctor."

I turned and looked at him. "The doctor would say it's just nightmares and to go home."

He pulled me into an embrace. Looking me in the eyes, he softened his voice and said, "I think you're wrong—I really do think the doctor is the best thing for you right now."

He was right, but I wasn't going to tell him that, so I gave him a quick kiss on the lips and said, with as much enthusiasm I could muster, "Thank you, but it's time for work."

He shook his head. As we parted, he said coldly, "Why do I even bother to help?"

I started to say something, but he grabbed his jacket and said, "Bye."

I listened as he made his way down the stairs and slammed the front door behind him. I fell onto my bed and burst into tears. I wanted to go after him but what would I say? *You're right, but I still think the doctors would say I'm crazy?*

Wiping the tears from my face, I headed downstairs. Regardless of how I felt, I still had to go to work.

* * *

Sitting at my desk, I looked out of the window at the beautiful weather. *Why am I in work?* Suddenly, a beep in my ear told me a call had come through. I dealt with the call, but honestly, it was mind-numbingly boring doing the same type of calls one after the other. This continued for about another hour, then it was time for my break. Finally, fresh air and food. First, I needed a fag and quick, before I snapped at someone.

In the fag shed, I met my colleague, Clare.

"You look like crap," she said.

I gave a half smile. "Thanks for that, but I do feel like shit. I was up all night, and then my boyfriend and I had a fight and he stormed off."

Clare smiled and said cheekily, "Tell me all the dirty details before the fight!"

I couldn't help but laugh slightly. "I wish there was something to tell, but nothing happened. We fought when he got to my place and continued this morning."

She put out her fag. "Too bad—I could have done with some juicy gossip. Maybe next time. Have to go back in now but see you later."

Then I was alone, finishing my cigarette. The argument lingered in my mind. I took my phone out of my pocket and rang Mason. There was no answer.

I went back inside to get some food. As I ate alone in the canteen, it dawned on me that today was going well compared to yesterday, much to my relief. Having said that, I really could not wait to leave and get home.

I left the canteen and walked down the long, empty corridor towards the stairs. It was too quiet. Suddenly, a chill rushed down my spine. I quickly turned around, but no one was there. I kept walking. After only two steps, I heard a noise but still could not see anything, so I carried on. As I turned the corner, there were footsteps behind me, but when I turned around a second time, no one was there. The footsteps were getting louder and louder. I quickened my pace. A whistling sound came along with the footsteps and I ran towards the door. I pushed the door open, letting it shut behind me, pulse pounding. Seeing people on the other side, and the staircase back to my floor, I released a shaking breath. The footsteps and whistling had stopped. I was safe. I ran up the stairs, trying to shake off the experience.

* * *

After a long day, I headed towards the train station. It was getting darker—soon it would be time for the clocks to go back. I loved the thought of putting the fire on and getting into my pyjamas early because of the weather, but I hated walking in the darkness, especially to the train station. However, it would be another month before it was properly dark on my walk home.

Finally there, waiting for my train, I noticed I was alone. According to my watch, it was only six o'clock. Had I missed the train? It didn't matter, one would be here within ten minutes and there'd be more people here soon.

I heard footsteps and, when I looked, there was someone coming to wait for the train. A train quickly passed on the other side of the platform and, when it was gone, that eerie feeling swept over me. When I glanced to my left, the figure was standing next to me, expressionless.

I quickly walked away. He followed me. My heart raced. I heard the train and turned around. He was gone. I got on the train and took a seat.

Out of the window, the scenery changed. I was starting to drift off when, in the window, I saw that figure sitting opposite me. I turned from the window and faced forward, not wanting to turn my head and see if the figure was real. Terror rose inside me.

A voice whispered, "You can't hide forever. You are next."

"What have I done?" I screamed. By now, I was freaking out, facing an empty seat. Other people looked at me. I was shaking and terrified—was I seeing things or was this real? One thing I knew, I wanted it to stop.

CHAPTER 4

A little girl ran, screaming for her parents. She looked terrified, but I couldn't move to help, only watch. Now we were in the living room; the television was on but no one was there. It must have been late as it was dark outside. I watched this child stop and stare at the screen. For a moment, she was silent, and then a piercing scream came from her lips. Her parents came running into the room. I tried to see what she was watching on the screen, but her parents distracted me. I couldn't believe it—they were *my* parents. When I looked again, the little girl was me.

My hands shook, trying to hold my drink. *I'm daydreaming.* I sat there, trying to work out if this was a real memory, but I couldn't. I tried to ring my mum, but I remembered that she was on a girls' weekend away, so I tried ringing my dad. As usual, it went to voicemail.

I left a message. "Hi, Dad. It's me, Em. This is going to sound weird, but did I suffer nightmares as a child, especially after watching television? Let me know. Thanks." It had to be one of the stupidest messages ever left on a voicemail, but hopefully it wouldn't freak my dad out too much.

I put some washing on and tried to have another drink when my dad called back.

"Hi, Dad."

"What was that voicemail you left me?" His voice was concerned.

I sighed and explained again. His response

was, "All children have nightmares, including you, but nothing out of the ordinary that I can remember. Although I bought something… now what was it… I can't remember at the moment, but you screamed and cried and it had to go in the bin."

"I don't remember anything like that; how long ago?" I waited eagerly for a response, hoping it would solve the mystery.

"Let's see, you were four or five at the time… trying to remember but can't. However, if I remember, I will let you know."

"Thanks, Dad—" I went to say something else, but Dad interrupted.

"Are you alright?"

I smiled as I answered. "I am, but I wanted to know if it was real or not."

He sighed. "Try asking your mother."

"I will. When are you getting back together?"

Dad stayed silent for a moment, then said, "I don't know that we will, Emily."

I wanted to talk more, but Dad made his excuses and hung up. I tried ringing Mason, but there was still no answer, so I decided to take a bath.

I slipped into a nice warm bath and let the bubbles do their work. Finally, I started to relax. I closed my eyes and pulled more bubbles towards me, drifting off. I heard a crash. Was someone trying to break into the house? I quickly got out the bath, grabbing my robe. I opened the door to be met by total darkness. I felt along the left side of the wall for the light switch and turned it on. In the light, everything looked like it should.

I slowly made my way down the stairs. I checked the living room, the kitchen, the dining room, but nothing seemed out of place. The only thing different was that my home looked like Blackpool illuminations. As I started turning lights off, I heard a whisper.

"I'm coming for you."

"Who are you?" I shouted as loud as I could.

The silence was tearing me apart. At this point, I didn't know which was worse: that creepy shadow of a man or these whispering voices. I wished I had seen his face, but it was always blurry. I wished I didn't live alone.

Maybe Mason was just trying to creep me out. However, the more I thought about it, the more I thought it was a ridiculous idea.

I needed noise in the house. I put the television on in the living room and pulled the blanket on the back of the sofa over me. I flicked through the channels and put on a comedy to watch. I started to laugh as the comedy continued. My eyes grew heavy and I slowly drifted off to sleep.

Pain shot through me, tearing my eyes open, and I screamed. The sofa was gone—I was on the floor. I raised my hand to the source of the pain. It felt wet. When I brought my hand before my eyes, I saw blood. My blood.

I glanced left, saw my house, and it dawned on me that I was outside. Suddenly, a sharp pain came again. I looked up. The man with no face was stabbing me. I tried to fight, but he was too strong and kept me in place with ease. When I realised there was no point struggling, I begged him to stop and leave me alone. The knife stabbed into me, again and again, quick and bloody. Through all this, my pleas went unheard.

CHAPTER 5

The following morning felt like a normal day after the last night's horror. It had felt so real, just like the other times. I looked at the ashtray, and it seemed I had smoked my way through a few fags. I couldn't blame myself though.

The doorbell rang. *Go away...* I needed to figure out what was going on, but I went to the door. When I opened it, all I could see was a bouquet of flowers, and then Mason's face came from behind them. "Sorry I snapped."

I smiled, accepted the flowers, and let him in. "They're beautiful, Mason. Thank you."

"How have you been?" he asked.

I pulled a vase out from the cupboard and started arranging the flowers. "I had a shitty night, but I'm good."

After his reaction last time, I wouldn't tell him any more. He didn't press for any more information either.

After a silence, he asked, "Are you ready for the party tonight?"

Surprise flashed through me. "That's tonight?"

He smiled. "Do you know what you are wearing?"

I looked at him with concern. "I don't know... Oh my god, what if I need a new outfit?"

Mason laughed, but for me, this was just the distraction I needed. A few days ago, I hadn't wanted to go to this, but at this point I'd take any distraction.

I ran upstairs, leaving Mason behind, but

before long he entered my room. As I tried to pick out what to wear, his hands were all over me. I tried to stop his hands wandering, but it was no use, so I faced him and asked, "What are you doing?"

He looked at me with hungry eyes that said it all and softly replied, "Well, if you're going to try a few outfits on before the party, I thought I would offer the help."

I kissed him. "We have all day yet."

He smiled that cheeky grin. "Good."

One thing led to another, until all my clothes were left forgotten on the floor and we were in bed. For a while, the nightmares felt so far away. When I looked at my clock on my side table it read three o'clock. I bolted out of bed, waking Mason up.

"If you hadn't distracted me then we wouldn't have fallen asleep."

Mason smiled. "Well, I heard no complaints, and on the plus side, you got some sleep."

"Glad you can see the funny side. Now I only have four hours to get ready!"

Mason offered to make a drink while I panicked over getting ready. I heard him come in and put the cup of tea down, but he didn't say anything because he knew I would only yell at him, so he left me to it. The television turned on in the living room as I carried on getting ready.

Finally, a few hours later, I came downstairs, ready.

Mason smiled. "You look sexy. I hope you won't mind, but I think I'll stay tonight so I can help you remove that dress."

I felt myself turn a shade of red. "Maybe, but shouldn't you get ready?"

"I'll be down in ten."

I smiled at the thought of that night. Within ten minutes, Mason was downstairs and ready.

* * *

We walked into the party and Mason introduced me to his colleague and friend, David.

"Hi, Emily. Glad you could come. Mason is always talking about you."

I blushed and looked at Mason.

"Em, don't listen to him." He grabbed my hand and pulled me away, giving David the evil look of *wait till we're in work*.

"Mason, you know, it's OK that you talk about me. I just hope it is all good."

He pulled me close and whispered in my ear. "Always."

Suddenly, the music was louder and I found myself shouting to talk. After a while, I asked where the bathroom was and Mason said, "Up the stairs and second on your right."

There was a downstairs toilet but another guest beat me to it, so I made my way upstairs. I was finishing up when the door handle kept going and a voice said, "Fucking hurry up."

I opened the door, but before I saw who was there, long fingernails wrapped themselves around the door. All the fear consumed me and I ran downstairs, pushing past people, and out the front door.

I rushed to the car and was frantically trying to open the door when Mason came out to find me.

"Em!" He shouted. "Em, look at me."

I turned to face him.

"The guy that freaked you out saw your reaction and told David, who then came and found me. Apparently, every time he comes to David's parties, he puts on the Freddy Krueger hands to see how many people he can frighten, but he's never seen someone so freaked out as you."

"Well, I don't think it was funny. After the nightmares I've been having, the stupid stunt he pulled has shaken me up."

"He's sorry. Now let's go back inside."

Angry, I pushed Mason away. "You can stay, but I'm leaving!"

"Fine, leave, but I'm staying. It was a bit of harmless fun and you need to lighten up. Learn to take a joke."

"If it was a joke, I'd be laughing," I snapped back. "You want to stay, fine, but when you're done, don't bother coming to mine as I can take my own dress off!"

Mason looked angry. "Fine by me. See you whenever."

CHAPTER 6

The way I slammed my front door, I thought the hinges would come away. I threw myself on the sofa and tried to calm down. I tried to play devil's advocate and see it from Mason's side, but I couldn't. The people at the party might have thought I was overreacting, but if they'd seen what I had or dreamt my dreams, they'd know where I was coming from.

My mobile rang. When I looked at the ID, it was Mason. Well, I wouldn't answer. I wasn't ready for another row, so I let it ring out.

A few minutes later, a text came through: *come back to the party and have fun*. He had a nerve; there was no apology, or an *are you alright*. He was probably drunk now or getting there. I turned my mobile off and went to bed to get a good night's sleep.

A loud bang woke me, and then the doorbell kept ringing. Looking at the time, it was four o'clock. I put my dressing gown on and, from the top of the stairs, shouted, "Who's there?"

The letter box swung open and a voice said, "It's fucking cold out here, and I left my house keys here at your place." It was Mason, who—surprisingly—didn't sound drunk.

Still at the top of the stairs, I shouted back, "Sure you left your keys here. Now go home."

"You can check if you want. They're on the hall table."

I looked over the banister and his keys were

right there. I went to the front door and, before I opened it, I said through the door, "I'm still pissed off at you."

His voice became quieter. "That guy started being horrible about you, so I punched him."

"Was that before or after you sent the text?"

He sighed. "After I sent the text. He started saying horrible things, and I just couldn't help but punch him. Then I left. I went home but realised I didn't have my key, and then walked around for a bit before coming here."

I opened the door and he walked in. He took my hand and led me upstairs. I got into bed while he undressed. Once he got under the covers, he pulled me close. "I should have left with you. Love you."

I glanced up at him. "I love you too."

* * *

I woke up to Mason getting out of bed. "Where are you going?"

He looked at me. "I have to work today."

I was surprised. "Isn't it your day off?"

He sat on the bed next to me. "It was supposed to be, but I got a call this morning saying that the duty manager is sick and because I'm the store manager, I have to go in."

"That sucks."

He got up and checked in the mirror that his black suit was tidy, then looked back to me. "Can we have a quiet night in and no arguments?"

I smiled at him. "That would be nice. I hate fighting."

He opened the bedroom door, turned back and blew me a kiss before leaving for work. I lay in bed for another hour before I couldn't stay there any longer.

While I was getting dressed, the doorbell went. I quickly threw something on and went downstairs to find my dad at the door. As I walked to the kitchen to make him a drink I asked, "So what brings you here?"

I noticed that Dad had lost weight since living separately from Mum, and I had to admit he looked better for it.

"After we talked the other day, I remembered what the item was."

I was still making the drink. "Do you still take sugar in your tea?"

"Yes, please." He answered me while making himself comfortable on a dining chair. The dining room and kitchen were only separated by an archway. "As I was saying, the item I'd bought was an armoured helmet. It had a small slit for the mouth, and when I poked my tongue out, that was when you screamed."

I placed his tea next to him and sat down with my drink. "So you poked your tongue through this slit and I screamed?"

He took a sip of his tea before putting his cup down and answering. "That's right. You were so upset that it couldn't stay in the house."

Disappointment settled in me. This didn't explain my nightmares. I'd been to museums and watched documentaries where people wore armour, and I was fascinated by the stories and how people could wear it as it looked so heavy. I considered it for a moment. This wasn't the answer.

"Thanks, Dad, but I don't think this helps."

He smiled at me. "Well, I was passing, so I thought I'd stop by and let you know. Where's Mason?"

"In work. Someone fell ill so he had to go in."

Dad finished his tea. "I have to shoot off, but you'll have to bring Mason over for dinner soon."

I kissed him goodbye. "We'll come over soon."

He opened his car door and replied, "Sooner rather than later, Emily."

"Bye, Dad." And with that, I closed the front door.

CHAPTER 7

Mason was due at mine in an hour and I wanted this evening to go well. I'd made cottage pie and hoped we could talk rather than argue. While I waited for him to knock, I lit a cigarette. A noise came from upstairs. I went to investigate and followed the noises to the spare room. I say spare room, but it was really an extension of my room because it was full of my clothes. When I opened the door, the television was on and clothes were on the floor. I couldn't remember making a mess, but maybe I'd got dressed in a hurry so I could start making food. However, the television I didn't remember turning on. It was only in there for when I had guests, like my parents or brother. I turned it off and heard a whisper.

"You shouldn't have done that; my favourite film was about to start."

I frantically looked around, but no one was there. Was my mind playing tricks on me? All I knew was that I had to know for sure. I started tearing the room apart; clothes flew as I pulled them from the drawers. Then I shoved cupboards forward to look behind them. I also unplugged the television and checked that too.

I don't know what I was expecting to find, but this nightmare I was living had to end and the sooner the better. But I found nothing—no wires, no nothing. I thought I'd find a tape with that creepy voice on it but nothing like that was in the room. Someone was out to get me, but who would do something like this, and why?

It could have been Mason. I never had nightmares when he was here...oh wait, yes, I did, after we argued and I told him to sleep on the sofa. What was wrong with me? I was accusing my boyfriend of purposely putting me through this hell.

My mobile rang, and the ID read Mason. When I answered, he asked, "You OK? I rang the doorbell several times and no answer."

"I'll be right there." Still on the phone, I made my way down the stairs.

When I opened the door, he kissed me.

"Where were you?" he asked.

We headed to the kitchen and I told him. "I thought I heard something in the spare room, but it wasn't anything. But before I realised it was nothing, I messed the room up a bit." It wasn't a complete lie, but I wasn't going to add '*by the way, I'm hearing voices*' into the mix. Mason would be calling the madhouse before I could finish explaining.

He poured us each a glass of wine and started to tell me about his day. "We've had Halloween and Christmas stock delivered today."

I looked at him with dismay. "What! It's only September."

Mason laughed at me as he took a bite of food. "Em, in the retail world, this isn't early. This is how it goes. After Christmas and New Year, we'll get a delivery for Easter."

I shook my head. "I don't care what season it is; it's just too early."

He smiled. "Personally, I agree, but this is retail for you. How was your day?"

I told him about Dad popping over and asking if we would come over for dinner.

"I'm off on Saturday—maybe we can go out for a meal. Have your parents talked since the split?"

I knocked back my glass of wine. "I wish they would. They're being very stubborn and driving me and Mark nuts."

"How is Mark?" I'd almost finished another glass of wine, so Mason added, "Slow down or there won't be any wine left for me."

I put the glass down. "Sorry. I just want Mum and Dad to sort things out, and when I try and call Mark there's no answer, not in the last couple of weeks anyway. I know he's just started to see someone."

Mason scooped a forkful of food and asked, "Didn't he just go through a break-up?"

I laughed. "In Mark's book, a week being single is long enough. Besides, I doubt he's serious about her. In fact, I can't ever see him getting married. How's Paul?"

"My brother loves married life and he keeps telling me to try it."

Had he just said what I thought he said? The M word? Now I had to ask. "Are you thinking about that? Marriage? I mean, with us?"

Mason looked shocked at my question. "I... um... Well, I have thought about it, but I don't think either of us is there yet, are we?"

Typical, put this on me. "I've thought about it, but when I think I'm ready... I don't think I am, you?"

Mason just kept looking at me, then said, "Em, I love you, but we've only been dating a year."

I don't know why, but his statement upset me. I got up and started clearing the dishes, literally taking Mason's plate from him, even though he evidently hadn't finished. I was stacking the dishwasher when I felt his arms wrap around me.

"I didn't say never, and with us arguing a lot lately, I would rather be sure. My parents divorced when I was a teenager, and it was hard on me and Paul. We only got to see Dad on weekends, and we were close."

I turned and faced him, still in his embrace. "It's just the way you said it—like you saw no future for us."

He kissed me softly. "I think about you, and us, all the time, and I want to see how things go between us."

I deepened the kiss, and things were starting to heat up when I heard, "Enjoy it while you can." A laugh followed.

I pulled away from Mason. "Did you hear that?"

He looked at me, puzzled. "Hear what? Because all I can remember was us kissing, and it was about to get interesting." He tried to pull me back for a kiss, but I pulled away.

"What I heard was real."

Mason said something, but all I heard was that voice, "You want to know if you're crazy? Maybe, maybe not," followed by that laugh.

I screamed in fear and tears ran down my face. "Fucking leave me alone!"

Then, as if I snapped out of a trance, Mason looked at me angrily. "Fine, I'll leave you alone. And here I was, thinking we were having a good night."

I chased after Mason, but by the time I caught up to him, the car was driving away.

CHAPTER 8

I woke up in the middle of the night after what could only be described as a restless sleep. I looked at my mobile. There were no missed calls or texts. Needing a drink, I headed for the stairs. I turned on the light and, when I got to the top of the stairs, a shadow walked past the downstairs corridor. I shouted out, but there was no answer.

I made my way slowly down the stairs, keeping my back against the wall. When I got to the bottom, I stretched out my arm and switched the light on. I looked around the corner. There was nothing there.

I went to the kitchen and was making that drink when the phone rang. It was almost three-thirty in the morning—who in their right mind would be ringing? I held back from answering for a moment then thought, *I live here, and I should not be afraid to answer my own phone*. When I answered, there was silence on the other end, so I shouted down the phone, "Stop calling," and I hung up. My hands were shaking—I couldn't take this anymore.

I rang Mason. It was a while, but when he answered the phone, it sounded like I had woken him up.

"Mason, I'm sorry. Please can you come over?"

He didn't sound pleased. "I'm confused about you at the moment. I asked if you were OK, and you swore at me and asked me to leave. So, no offence, but I think I'll stay home."

"Please," I begged.

"I show concern, and all you do is throw it back in my face. Up until a few weeks ago, things were fine. Now you're imagining things and talking to yourself..."

By that point, I was crying down the phone, trying to speak, but I couldn't form the words.

"Night, Em." And with that, he hung up.

I was still crying while I held the phone in my hand. I needed him—really needed him. This was my low point; I couldn't be here alone. Fingers trembling, I redialled his number, holding my breath until he answered.

"What, Em?"

I tried to hold the tears back. "Please come over—I'm scared."

Mason was still angry when he replied. "I was there, but you told me to fuck off, so why should I come back?"

I couldn't explain why. I just said, "Please. I need you."

There was silence for a few minutes, then Mason replied, "Fine, I'll be there shortly. But when I do, I'm there for the night."

I was so relieved, I just answered, "Thank you."

Twenty minutes later, Mason was at my door. When I tried to hug him, he grabbed my arms.

"We need to talk," he said.

We went into the living room and he sat beside me on the sofa. He placed his hands over mine and said firmly, "I want to know what is going on, and I don't want to hear it is nothing."

My eyes were heavy from when I had been crying earlier, so I took a deep breath.

"I'm sorry, Mason..." I said softly.

He looked at me, raising his eyebrow. "I know you are sorry, but you aren't telling me anything. If you don't, I will leave."

I started to shake. "That's just it, Mason—I'm not sure what's wrong. It started with this dream, and it hasn't stopped…"

He looked puzzled. "Tell me about the dream?"

I looked away. "I can't, because you'll think I'm crazy…"

He turned my head so we faced each other. "Em, we're already there. So talk."

I explained everything—from the first dream that had felt so real, through every variation, and the one where I'd thought he'd been killed.

Mason looked shocked and squeezed my hand. "You should have said something sooner. Is there anything else?"

I glanced away. "I'm hearing voices, seeing things, but I have no idea if they're real or not." And then I started crying again.

Mason's strong arms wrapped around me, and his voice softened as he quietly said, "You aren't going to work tomorrow, and neither will I. Hopefully we can figure this out together."

I tried to protest about work, but Mason gave his angry stare so I decided not to argue.

* * *

When I woke up and went downstairs, Mason was nowhere to be found. I was heading back upstairs when the front door opened and he walked in with a suitcase.

"I hope you don't mind, but I took your house key to let myself back in."

I was still looking at the suitcase when he added, "I decided the best thing would be to keep you company, so I'm moving in temporarily until we know what's wrong."

I didn't remember being asked if I was OK with

this. I'd been in a state the previous night, but shouldn't we have discussed this?

I went to speak, but he said, "I think this is for the best. By the way, I had a spare key cut as well."

CHAPTER 9

Since Mason started staying over, I'd had a really good few days, but this nagging doubt remained, in the back of my mind, that he might have had something to do with everything that had been happening. A few things made me think that. Firstly, the other night, when I'd phoned and begged him to come over, I'd just received a silent phone call and, for all I knew, Mason had set me up. The second reason was that he could have rigged my spare room, but how? I'd found nothing. I'd always been told to go with my instinct and, right then, it was telling me something was not right. My bedroom looked like a bomb had hit it... The bed was a mess and whenever I went to the bathroom, the toilet seat was left up all the time. There were dirty dishes in the sink, even though the dishwasher was right there, under the sink—and don't get me started on my living room.

However, despite all this, Mason being there had calmed me down. The nightmares were slowing right down and the voice I'd been hearing had stopped, so that was a good thing, right?

Mason insisted I should continue to stay off work. When I said I thought he was right and that I should see a doctor, he firmly told me that I shouldn't—I'd be wasting their time, and we would get through this together. When I tried to question his reasoning and insist that maybe I should, he firmly said, "I just told you, Em, that you don't need to see the doctor. Besides, you're getting better."

Later that night, I lay in bed as Mason slept. I kept wondering if he was behind all my nightmares and why he didn't want me to go to work or see a doctor. I quickly came to the conclusion that I needed to talk to my doctor before I returned to work. Finally, I felt better, so I decided to get answers for myself. A weight had been lifted from me and I closed my eyes, drifting off to a peaceful sleep.

I woke to find myself standing outside my house. It was cold, and the ground was wet from where it had been raining. Suddenly, something pushed me to the ground. When I tried to get up, I couldn't. I managed to turn around. A male figure stood over me. As he moved closer, the moonlight fell across his face. I gasped, stunned. It was Mason, and there was a knife in his hand. He just stared at me as he started to stab me. I cried for him to stop, even managed to ask why. He raised the knife again, my own blood dripping from it.

"Are you mad?" he said. "Maybe."

Then he plunged the knife into me, and I closed my eyes.

I woke up, sweat pouring from me. I was alive. Mason held me, but I pushed him away and quickly got out of the bed.

"Em, you're white as a sheet..."

I didn't let him finish. "Why are you doing this? Why did you stab me?"

He looked baffled. "Em, I haven't done anything to you. If you look, you haven't been stabbed! You're fine!"

I slowly looked at myself. He was telling the truth. "I saw you, Mason, as clear as I see you now. You stabbed me and said what I heard the voice say—'*Are you mad? Maybe.*'—so don't tell me I'm making it up, because I'm not."

He thought about what I'd said, then answered, "I haven't stabbed you—I wouldn't hurt you. But at least now, you're talking to me."

What a lame thing to say, was all I could think. "Well, I'm making an appointment to see the doctor." I didn't want to hear his reply, so I added, "Thank you for staying, but I need to have my house back."

He looked at me with a blank expression, which I found odd. "I'm not leaving…" he said.

Why wasn't he listening? "This is my house," I said firmly, "and you have your own place, so you need to leave."

Mason got out of bed and started to get dressed. "I know this is your place, but you aren't right and keep calling me when you get frightened by these nightmares, so I'm staying. End of story."

CHAPTER 10

When I contacted the doctors, I couldn't believe there were no appointments available for six weeks. Even when I explained to the receptionist what was going on, they advised that if it wasn't an emergency then I would have to wait. I was going through hell—if this wasn't an emergency, then I didn't know what was.

The doorbell rang, but Mason got the door before I did. Mum loved Mason, and she greeted him with a big smile. When she entered the living room, where I was sitting, she said, "Are you living together now?"

I rolled my eyes at her. "No, Mum, we're not living together, and no, before you ask, we're not engaged."

She smiled at me. "So why are you not in work?"

I would have tried to lie to her, but she would have seen through it. "I've been having nightmares—that's all."

Then she said something that threw me off guard. "You used to have lots of nightmares when you were younger, but I thought you'd outgrown them."

I bolted upright as Mason walked in with a coffee for my mum. "What nightmares?"

She took a sip of the coffee. "It was about someone chasing you," she said calmly, "but you never saw their face."

You could have picked my mouth up off the

floor. Mason looked at my mum, waiting patiently for more information.

"You both look in shock," she said. "Emily, are they the same nightmares?"

I couldn't speak, so I nodded.

"Has something happened to bring this back?"

I thought for a moment, then replied, "Dad told me about an armour helmet and that I screamed."

Mum smiled. "Your dad didn't mean for you to be frightened, and because of that, he put it in the bin."

"He told me that. Mum, is there anything else?"

Mum was silent for a moment, then said, "Not that I can think of, but if I think of anything, then I'll let you know."

She went to leave, but I asked, "Are you hiding something from me? Both you and Dad have said similar things, and I get the feeling you're keeping something from me."

She turned back to face me. "Emily, I am not keeping anything from you. If I know anything, then you know."

I raised my voice. "You knew about the nightmares but never said a thing to me."

She sighed. "They stopped a long time ago, so until now, they weren't worth mentioning."

I wasn't happy with the answer. "What triggered the nightmares?"

"If I knew, I would tell you."

She was hiding something—I knew it—but I dropped it for now and watched her leave.

Once she had left, Mason said, "That was interesting."

"It was, but as I said before, you can leave and go back to your place."

He looked at me with concern. "I'll leave,

but I still think you need company. Call me if the nightmares happen again."

I smiled at him but couldn't help but wonder why he was suddenly being so understanding.

He gathered all his things and, within thirty minutes, he was by the front door. It felt so final, like we were breaking up, but it wasn't. I stood by the living room door, looking at him.

"You know I'm trying to help you?" he said.

"I want to believe, Mason, but I'm not sure," I said quietly as my hands fidgeted.

He tried to come close, but I backed away.

"Em, all I want you to do is talk to me. Help me understand."

I was starting to shake. "You wanted me to go to the doctors, but I said no," I said firmly. "But when I agreed to see them, you told me no. Why?"

Mason scratched the back of his head. "I don't know. Maybe I thought they wouldn't believe you, or…sorry, I have no answer. But if you want, I will come with you." He opened the door, but turned back to me and said softly, "For what it's worth, I do want to help."

After he closed the door, I started to clean the house to get rid of the mess he'd left behind. It took a few hours to get the house back to the way I liked it, and it felt good to accomplish so much. I was so happy I blasted music while I danced around, but after an hour, I collapsed on the sofa.

Tomorrow was a new day, and I was going to return to work. I needed normality, whatever that was.

When I headed off to bed, I went to open the bedroom door, and the floor creaked. No one was there, but as I turned the door handle, I heard, "Now let's have some fun."

CHAPTER 11

I froze on the spot, but no one was there.

"Who are you?" I yelled.

There it was, that horrible laugh, and then, "Does it matter? You tried to forget me, but I'm here to tell you that you can't. I'm too important. I am a part of you that will never let go, so go and run, but I'll always find you."

I raced down the stairs, frightened, shaking, tears running down my face. I ran from the house and jumped in my car for the first time in a few weeks and drove as far away as I could. For a while, I drove around, not sure of where I was going, until I pulled up outside Mason's home.

I was too shaken to move from my seat, so I just buried my head in the steering wheel and cried uncontrollably. Suddenly, the car door opened and I jumped. When the person bent down, it was Mason.

He looked at me with eyes wide with worry. "What happened?"

I couldn't tell him. The words didn't sound right due to all of my crying. When he realised that I couldn't communicate, he just pulled me in to an embrace. After a few minutes, he pulled me from the car and took me into his home. He sat me down, turned on the television, and I screamed suddenly when I saw the screen.

"Can you turn that off?" I said. "I've had enough scares for one night."

He picked up the remote and changed channel.

"I couldn't sleep so decided to watch a horror."

"I just can't take anymore tonight, that's all," I replied through the tears as I was calming down.

He slouched into his sofa and pulled me into him. "Can you tell me what happened now?"

As I lay on his chest, I explained what had happened, and he asked if I wanted to stay the night. I didn't say anything, but nodded and squeezed his hand.

"Em, do you know why this is happening?"

I didn't move but answered, "I really don't know, but I wish I did. Mason, I have to ask this… Are you trying to frighten me?"

"What?" Mason raised his voice, obviously hurt. "No, I wouldn't, and I can't believe you would think that."

"I ask because you have access to my home, and now you have a spare key," I said softly, sitting up to look at him. "You also insisted on staying and never asked if I was really OK with you being there. I mean, call me crazy, but what am I supposed to think?"

He glared at me. "You're supposed to trust me, remember? Your boyfriend? If you can't or won't trust me, how can we be together?" I went to say something, but he cut me off. "Do you want to be with me?"

"Yes, I do, but it seems sometimes you're there for me and at other times you're not."

Now Mason was angry. "I'm always there for you, but lately you're the one acting strangely, and when I try and help you get angry with me. You also push me away then ask for my help. It's like whatever I do, it's never good enough or I'm in the wrong. I want to help, but you aren't giving me any information."

I started to cry but pushed back the tears.

"You think this is fun for me? I fall asleep and see a no-faced man chase me and wake up and think it was real. Now I'm hearing voices. I see the same figure at my work, and it scares me…"

"The figure's at work?"

His look said it all. I stared at him, mind racing. *Shit, what did I just say? Crap, now how will I get out of this one? I forgot I hadn't told him about this…shit…shit…shit.*

Mason gave the look that said *I'm waiting for an explanation*, so I took a deep breath and said, "I saw the figure from my dreams in my workplace, and when I ran and got back inside, they asked if I was OK. I told them I wasn't well, but then it happened again in a quiet area of the building. That time, no one seemed to notice, thankfully."

Mason sat down. "When did this happen?" By now, he had lowered his voice. "You know what? Never mind, Em, because you should have told me. I can't help you when you withhold information."

I sat next to him. "Mason, I really don't know why this is happening, but please can I have your support?"

He smiled at me. "I will give you the help you need, but I do think you need company right now. You can move in here, or me there, or half and half."

I started to object once again. "I'm fine living on my own, really." By this point, I was trying to convince myself.

Mason folded his arms and replied in a firm tone, "I'm not saying you can't cope living on your own, but with what's going on right now, you need someone there. Look, if you don't want me, I get that, but you could live with your parents instead."

His suggestion horrified me. "I don't need my parents watching over me. I'm not a child!"

"Then if you don't want them, live with me temporarily."

I thought for a moment before replying. "I want to try one more time on my own—and before you say anything, I know I shouldn't, but I want to beat whatever this is. If I fail, then we'll change the living arrangements until we find out what is bothering me."

He held my hands. "I think you're being silly, but I do understand. However, if this happens again then I'll be stuck to you like glue."

I smiled at his sweet gesture and kissed him. The kiss intensified, and his arms took hold around my waist. I still had my doubts, but—and maybe it was the vulnerable part of me taking over—I wanted him so badly. I know the time was wrong, but I wanted normality. Believe me when I say this—after what I had been through, I was going to take it.

I leaned back as he kissed my neck and let his hands wander. A sudden tug told me he wanted my top gone. I raised my hands and he pulled the top upwards and threw it on the floor. I lost myself in the moment, until I was naked on the sofa with Mason inside me.

After we finished, we cuddled up, watching the television.

I heard a whisper. "Nice to be home?"

I went to get up, but Mason tightened his grip and kept me in place. I tried to turn around, but his grip was still strong. Then I heard that horrible laugh once more.

"You'll never be free now."

CHAPTER 12

After returning from Mason's, I sat down in my kitchen and replayed the previous night in my head. Randomly turning up at his house showed I trusted and felt safe with him, but his hold on me, and then that voice... Was it Mason putting on a voice? I'd had my back to him, so I hadn't seen his face, but he'd sounded so sincere when he said he wanted to help. I didn't know what to think, but I knew I wanted answers.

I opened up my laptop and Googled nightmares. It said what I had expected, that it was 'a frightening or unpleasant dream'. I clicked on night terrors. That seemed to define me at this point—'feelings of great fear on waking in the night.' But what was behind this?

I needed a distraction, so I put the television on. After a few minutes spent flicking through the channels, I settled on the comedy channel. I needed a laugh. The adverts were on, as usual, and I heard the post come through the letterbox so I went to get it. As I looked through the pile, I heard the voice that had been taunting me, but this time it was coming through the telly. I raced back to the living room, but the programme was just starting again. I tried to rewind back to the adverts to see what could have been responsible, but the remote wouldn't work. Of course—it had only worked intermittently since I'd spilt a drink on it. My mind started racing; what was on that advert? I fell onto my sofa and felt deflated.

I needed fresh air, so I went for a walk. I ended up in town and thought I would get a few things while I was there. After going into a few different shops, I remembered I needed to walk to the other end of town to get a birthday card for a friend at work. The walk always seemed long, even though it only ever took ten minutes to get there. As I walked past the shops, many of them were already advertising Halloween. It was the beginning of September but, as Mason had said to me, in retail it didn't matter. Each shop had an eerie window display, some very dark and sinister. My blood ran cold at the thought of the monsters coming alive as I passed, especially after my dreams and the voices I had heard, so I crossed the road to avoid being near them. Hopefully, once I solved the mysterious nightmares and voices, things like shop windows wouldn't bother me. I finished my shopping and went home.

As I got through the door, my phone rang. I raced into the living room and picked it up.

"Hello?"

"Do you ever answer your mobile?"

A smile crept over me face as I moved the bags out of the way to sit down. "Hi, Laura. What's up?"

"Where have you been?" She was the type who always got to the point. "Are you sick? Because you haven't been in work, and everyone is worried. Well, maybe not the boss, but then he never gives a shit about anyone. But I care."

"I just haven't been sleeping very well, and it's affecting me during the day, but I'll be back tomorrow, regardless."

"Good," Laura replied. "Otherwise, I'll have to get that birthday card, and you know I'm not good at getting things like that. Are you sure you're alright?"

I thought how to answer. "I'm alright." That was all I had to offer her.

"Fine—then I'll see you in the canteen before work."

"OK. See you then, Laura."

Hearing from my friend was just the boost I'd needed to make me feel better about returning to work. I took my shopping bags to the kitchen and unpacked them, sorting the shopping into piles so it would cut down on putting it all away. I always told myself that after shopping, so it never seemed to take long.

Once I'd settled down, there was a knock at the door. When I answered, there were two young teenagers there.

"Trick or treat?" they shouted.

I was puzzled—it was only September.

"I think you're a bit early," I said.

Their response was to throw flour at me and run away. I slammed the door shut. I saw myself in the mirror opposite the door—I was covered in flour. Stupid kids. Now I was going to have to jump in the shower and get cleaned up. This top was my favourite, so the flour had better come out of it.

I put my clothes in the washing machine and headed for the shower. As I stepped out of the shower, I heard the doorbell. I quickly put my dressing gown on and went to answer the door. When I opened it, no one was there. I closed the door and headed back upstairs to get changed. The doorbell went again. I answered again but, again, no one was there. This time, I stepped outside, but I couldn't see anyone, so I headed back inside. Maybe kids were playing knock, knock ginger.

I'd started to get dressed when the phone went. I stopped what I was doing and answered, but there was no one on the other end.

"Hello?" I kept saying. "Hello?"

There was no answer. Over the next hour, the phone rang again, and again, and again, and there was always silence on the other end. Each time, I dreaded it more. When the phone went again, I lost it, and shouted down the phone, "*Who are you*?!"

CHAPTER 13

I slammed the phone down and backed away. Then the doorbell rang.

"Go away!" I screamed.

There was a thud at the door, and a voice shouted, "Emily, open this door, please."

It was one voice I was glad to hear—my dad's. When I opened the door, I collapsed into his arms in tears. Before I knew what was happening, I was sitting on the sofa with a hot cup of tea in my hands.

Tears were still rolling down my cheeks when he asked, "What's wrong?"

I drank some of the tea and started to tell him everything. "Remember the nightmares I told you about?" Dad nodded as I continued, "They're getting worse. In one, I saw Mason stabbing me. I'm hearing voices… I thought I heard the voice on telly, but when I went to see what it was, the advert had finished. You told me about an armour helmet, and I thought I saw the figure from my dream on the street or in work. I think I might be crazy, Dad."

The look on his face showed he was digesting everything I'd told him.

"Mason…has he hurt you?" he asked.

Oh great—that was what my dad focused on. "Dad, he hasn't hit me, but I have thought he may be responsible for the voice because, before the advert, I'd pulled my spare room apart to find evidence. Then Mason practically moved in—"

Dad interrupted me. "Emily, I really don't think Mason would do this to you. I'm not saying you're wrong, but I just don't think he's capable. Are you two arguing a lot?"

I nodded. "We are, and it's horrible. I think what is happening is affecting us."

Dad didn't say anything but put his arms around me. After a while, I pulled away and asked, "What about the phone calls?"

"Probably just silent calls. They're horrible, but I don't think someone is out to get you. I would suggest going to the doctors and seeing what they say."

I tried to give a smile. "I'll try again, but last time they said there were no appointments for six weeks."

Dad suggested I nagged them to death until I got the appointment.

Once he'd left, I did feel a bit better, but those doubts still nagged me.

* * *

I met Laura in the canteen before work.

"Are you feeling better?" she asked.

I ate some of my breakfast and replied, "Not really, but I'm getting there."

Laura knew not to press any further. "There's a party in a few weeks—do you want to go?"

I shook my head. "I'll think about it. What type of party is it?"

"It's a Halloween party. Everyone's dressing up; music is going to be played by a live band so it should be really good."

I thought for a moment. "I'll think about it. Can partners go?"

"More the merrier! So yes, Mason can go."

She glanced at her watch. "We'd better get going, or we'll be late logging in."

Shit—she was right. Going back to work meant going back to reality.

* * *

I sat near the window while I took calls one after another. Each time a new call came through, my headset beeped in warning. However, my mind wasn't on my job today. There was too much going on that I didn't understand, and the last place I wanted to be was here, taking calls.

My team leader came over to do a back-to-work interview. I watched him talk to me and all I could think was, *Can I get back to my desk?* I considered telling the truth, but how could I explain when I still had no idea what the hell was going on? After about thirty minutes and a few verbal nods, I signed the relevant paperwork and went back to my desk.

When I left work, I was shocked to see Mason waiting for me.

"How have you been today?" he asked.

I smiled at him. "It's been a good day. Why are you here? I told you I wanted to try being on my own."

He took my hand and said, "I know what you said, but I'm worried about you."

I smiled at him. "Thank you, but really, I'm fine." There it was, another lie. In truth, I was scared and Mason could see that.

"Em, I'm going to take you home so we can talk more."

I felt like I was a child being scolded, but I knew that wasn't the case.

When we got home, Mason offered to make

the tea. I stood in the kitchen and waited for him to speak.

"So, are you going to talk or shall I start?" He sounded serious.

"You can start," I said.

"I'm sick of you pushing me away. I'll admit, at first, I didn't take what was happening seriously, but I am now. I'm not trying to drive you crazy or murder you and, after listening to your mother, I think she's holding something back. All this has got me thinking about us, and I think we should move in together permanently."

I sat down on the sofa, put my drink on the side table and digested what he had just said. "I'm not trying to push you away, but I'm in the dark just as much as you. Don't take this personally, but I don't know who I can trust. I agree my mum is hiding something and this hasn't helped with the trust issues I've had lately. I want to believe you aren't out to get me, and the only way that can be answered is to know what is wrong with me. Living together... Wow, that's new. I thought we were happy with the way things were."

Mason looked at me calmly. "Even though you've pissed me off lately, I want to know you're safe, and the more I think about it, the more I know living together would be the right thing—"

I interrupted him. "Safety...that's the reason why we need to live together? What about love, passion and can't be without each other? Wanting to spend twenty-four hours a day, seven days a week together and not apart? Due to the arguing, that's not how things are at the moment."

"I'll admit you're right, but I love you and worry about you more and more. Once we know what's wrong, then things with us will get back to normal."

I didn't want to talk about living together

anymore, so put the telly on. We watched it a while, and then Mason asked, "Do you want another drink?"

I nodded. "Yes, thanks."

He went to the kitchen, and after a few minutes I followed him. I grabbed my drink, and then I heard the voice again on the telly.

"I'll see you soon."

CHAPTER 14

I stared at the TV.

"What is it?" Mason asked.

My voice was shaking. "The voice I've been hearing was on the telly in an advert, but my remote doesn't work, so I can't rewind."

"It's OK—I'm here."

I tried to put on a brave face as we continued to watch the programme. After it finished, I went to the bathroom, and when I came back, Mason asked, "Is it OK if we watch *Scream*?"

"It's not one of those horror films, is it?" I asked.

He moved to the same sofa as me. "It's a horror and a comedy—it's not that bad."

I agreed, because otherwise he'd just carry on trying to persuade me. When the film started, all I remember is hiding my face, either behind a pillow or turning away. Then, without warning, while my head was turned, I heard the voice again. When I turned to face it, my blood ran cold. Scream was speaking into the phone, terrorising the person on the other end.

I squeezed Mason's arm. "That's the voice I've been hearing over and over," I said quietly.

"Are you sure?" Mason turned the film off.

I was shaking. "I'm sure, but I've never seen the film before. And how can you say it's part comedy? Because I saw nothing funny in what we watched." When Mason didn't say anything, I added, "I told you I don't like horrors. I'm going to bed. Night."

It wasn't long before Mason followed me upstairs.

"Are you OK?" he asked.

I looked at him. "I feel numb, but at least I know that I'm not crazy."

He sat on the edge of the bed. "You aren't crazy. Did you try ringing your mum?"

"I did, but no answer."

At that moment, I received a text message from my mum: *There is a programme on about childhood TV, you'll love it.* She gave me the channel. I told Mason and put on the TV in the bedroom, as my mum was sure to ask questions, and I'd have to tell her something. The programme did make me smile, and Mason and I both recognised shows as we watched. One I'd watched growing up was *Worzel Gummidge*. When they showed a clip, I laughed as it brought back good memories. My favourite character in the show had been Aunt Sally. My mum had bought me an 'Aunt Sally' mask—I remembered having it in my bedroom, and that there was something odd about it.

I sat there thinking about how at night, I used to cover the mask up under my chair, as if it didn't exist. I couldn't look at it and I could never touch it as it gave me the creeps. My mother thought I was crazy. She warned me she would bin it and, to her shock, I said, "Bin it then." Eventually, she did.

I tried to ring my mum, but there was no answer, so I texted her asking her to ring me ASAP.

"What's wrong?" Mason asked.

"I loved the show *Worzel Gummidge*, but I hated this Aunt Sally mask Mum bought me, and I made her get rid of it. That's why I was trying to ring her."

Mason pulled me close and said, "Hopefully she'll be able to answer your questions."

I thought about what he'd said for a moment and replied, "I really hope so, because I need the answers. Oh, by the way, Laura said there's a Halloween party in a few weeks and asked if I wanted to go. You can come with me."

Mason kissed my forehead. "That sounds like fun, and hopefully we'll have this all cleared up before we go."

This was good—Mason and I not arguing but getting on for once.

"Fun sounds like a plan," I said. "I haven't had much of that lately."

Mason squeezed me tightly. "We both need this, and it would make a change to always arguing."

We kissed passionately and said goodnight to each other. I felt so relaxed that I finally believed I would get a good night's sleep. For the first time in a while, there were no voices, the house felt calm and Mason and I were getting on. As I drifted off, my last thought was, *I just hope this isn't the calm before the storm*.

CHAPTER 15

When I came downstairs, Mason was already dressed.

"So, do you want a cuppa?" he asked me.

"Yes, please," I replied, smiling.

He looked at me while he waited for the kettle to boil. "Do you want a lift to work?"

"What time are you leaving?"

"In thirty minutes," Mason said, finishing off my tea.

I started to panic—I wasn't even dressed. "That doesn't give me much time," I said as I ran out the room.

Halfway up the stairs, I realised I'd left my tea in the kitchen, so I ran back down. When I entered the kitchen, Mason was holding my cup.

"Forgot this?"

"Thanks." I grabbed it from his hands and quickly ran back up the stairs.

* * *

As he drove me to work, Mason brought up the subject of moving in together.

"Em, what do you think?"

I had just finished smoking my cigarette and threw it out the window. "I don't know…" I said, closing the window. "I need time to think it through. Where would we live?"

"I live in a flat, so I could move into your house or we could get a place together that would be ours."

Shit—he had thought this through. He couldn't have just said something stupid; no, he had it all planned.

"Mason, let me think on it, OK?"

As he pulled up outside my work, he gave his cheeky smile and leaned over to kiss me goodbye.

"Think about it," he said, "and have a good day."

Flustered, my cheeks reddened and I couldn't explain why. "You too."

Inside, I'd just reached my desk when my team leader said, "Team meeting. Those who have just arrived, log in and then join the meeting."

I logged in, wishing we could just skip the happy team meeting and get back to work. Once all the team were together, my team leader started with what was going on within the company—how the stats looked for our team and the centre as a whole. I zoned out after a few minutes, then my team leader said, "As we are always looking to create a fun atmosphere, we are encouraging every team to decorate their space with Halloween decorations. It won't be long before it's here, so start thinking of ideas for our team area, and in a few weeks, we will start putting things up."

Some members of the team started to voice their ideas—a giant spider above our desks was one idea, another was using black bins bags to shape a grotto-style entrance.

Suddenly, my team leader looked at me and asked, "Emily, any ideas?"

Great—he was asking me. Just what I needed. My response was a simple, "Nope…no ideas yet." I hoped that would be enough for him to stop asking me.

Shortly after this, my team leader told us to return to the phones.

As I took a call, the others in the team were still talking about decorations. When I had finished, one team member asked me, "What do you think?"

I looked at him and replied, "I was talking to a customer so didn't hear all the conversation, but when we had the team meeting the grotto bit sounded good."

That was it, the boys on the team started talking how they could put a Halloween grotto together at our desks. The girls talked about dressing up and the make-up they would need. I loved a good party, but mixing work and fun like this never went well. It probably didn't help that I didn't like my job. All I was thinking was *roll on home time*.

* * *

My mobile rang while I was on the train. I didn't look at the ID, just pressed accept.

It was my mum.

"Do you remember the Aunt Sally mask you bought me?" I asked.

"I remember. I bought you the mask and you didn't like it, so I threw it out. Why?"

I explained about the film.

"You were a child when you had the Aunt Sally mask," Mum said, "and most people don't like horrors, so I wouldn't worry about it."

She was probably right but I still had that feeling. I was in the middle of talking when the line dropped as I went through a tunnel. Suddenly, in the darkness of the tunnel, I saw that figure from my dream in the window. He sat opposite me, running his hand up and down his knife's blade. I was freaking out, but I forced myself to stay calm. When I turned around, the figure was gone.

CHAPTER 16

When I got off the train, I was still shaken, so I went to the bathroom at the station. The toilet door was slatted. I wasn't convinced I'd have any privacy, but my bladder wouldn't wait any longer.

Suddenly, the outer door creaked open. I was trapped in the small cubicle. A flurry of thoughts ran in my head: *Is this figure real? Has he found me? Will I be dead within a few minutes?*

The door creaked again so I waited a few minutes before bravely unbolting the door and venturing towards the sink. The bathroom was empty, and I was alone. I quickly left the bathroom, even more anxious than I'd been on the train. Suddenly, I heard the creaking again. As I turned around, a man left the men's bathroom. It finally dawned on me—the sound hadn't come from the bathroom I'd been in.

My mind had to be playing tricks on me, but the question was why? I needed to think, so when I got home I started cleaning my bedroom. I thought about everything that had happened over the last few weeks, but nothing stood out. Yes, there were little things, but nothing that said *THIS IS WHY!* on a big sign.

I stopped for a minute. The house was so quiet with no music and no television on. In fact, I would go as far as to say it felt eerie. Suddenly I had this feeling of panic. I looked outside my bedroom door and it was dark, so I quickly put the hall light on to brighten things up. Then I put the TV on to create noise before going back to tidying my room.

I was making good progress when the stairs creaked. All my senses told me something was wrong, but I was frozen to the spot, unable to move. Dread filled my body. I had nothing to hand to defend myself with.

I waited and watched as my door started to open, fingers appearing around the frame, then a foot. I was about to scream, when Mason appeared in the doorway with bags in his hands.

"You fucking ass!" I shouted as I threw clothes at him.

He looked shocked. "I did call out, but no one answered."

I noticed he had a duffel bag with him. "What have you got in there?" I said.

"A few more clothes, and don't start on me—all I want is to help."

I picked up the clothes I had thrown. I had a few words I wanted to say, but he was right. Things were getting weird and, for whatever reason, fear was starting to control me. As much as I hated to admit it, I needed someone.

"I suppose you'll want a drawer to put them in?" I said sarcastically.

"That would be nice." I was looking away, so he held my arm. When I looked at him, he softly added, "When this is all over, I promise, if you want me to go home, I will."

I gave half a smile. "Sorry—it's just that I want answers, but I'm scared."

He wrapped his arms around me. "I know, and that's why I'm here. Do you fancy going out tonight?"

I looked at him in shock. We hadn't been out with just the two of us in ages. I smiled in agreement.

Mason left the room. As I cleared out a drawer,

a noise came from behind me. The lamp was on the floor, luckily still intact. How had it got there? I was alone in the bedroom and no windows were open, so there'd been no gust of wind to knock it over.

I placed it back on the side table. I opened the duffel bag and started to put Mason's clothes away. Without warning, I felt sick. As I looked in the duffel bag, my body froze; I couldn't take my eyes off it. I wanted to scream, but no sound could escape my lips. My legs gave way from under me and I fell to the floor. I was in survival mode as I scrambled backwards and hit my chest of drawers. I scrambled around to pull myself up. I slid sideways along the chest of drawers and then against the wall, trying to make my escape, but all the while keeping an eye on the duffel bag. Now the fear was growing inside me, and I felt cold even as sweat poured down my face. All I could think was I needed to get out of my bedroom.

CHAPTER 17

I ran down the stairs and out the front door. I don't think I even closed it, but I didn't care. Now I understood everything—Mason was behind all this. The hurt broke my heart in two as I loved him so much. All I could do was run and keep running, and the further away the better. My home was tainted by his twisted plan, whatever that was.

He called out to me, but I wasn't going to listen. I flagged down a taxi coming up the road, and dived in, shouting, "Just go!" The driver must have picked up that I was scared, because he put his foot down. As the taxi drove past, Mason looked shocked and puzzled to say the least.

* * *

When I arrived at my dad's, he didn't seem surprised to see me. I walked into the living room and Mason was sitting in a chair.

"Are you alright?" he said.

I was shaking and raised my voice, "I want you as far away from me as possible."

Before Mason could respond, Dad intervened, "Emily, what's wrong?"

"I was unpacking his bag to put the clothes in the drawer, and halfway through the bag, a long knife was just sitting there. It made me feel sick."

Dad looked at Mason and demanded he explain himself.

Mason didn't flinch. "Em...hun, did you pick the knife up?" he asked calmly.

"It was a fucking *knife*, why would I pick it up?!" I shouted.

He was still calm, which irritated me even more. "Em, it's a plastic knife. I got it because it looks real. Remember the Halloween party we're going to? Well, it will go with my Jason costume from *Friday the 13th*. When the guy in the shop showed me the knife and I saw how real it looked, I couldn't resist."

"And you can prove this?" Dad asked.

"Dad..." I firmly said.

"Em, I will come back to your house with both of you, and that way he can prove what he's saying and, if he's lying, then we call the police and kick him out."

"And what if he swaps the knife while we are downstairs?"

"I'll go with Mason to see this knife. Mason, do you object?"

Mason shook his head. "I'm fine with this."

"Good, let's go."

* * *

I stood in my bedroom doorway, and everything was the way I'd left it. Maybe Mason had done something? While I stood there, my dad and Mason entered the room.

My dad glanced over into the bag. "Did you see a knife?" he said.

"Yes," I said impatiently. "See? He wants to—"

Dad cut me off in the middle of my sentence by showing me the knife. "Emily, it looks very real, I won't doubt that, but when I try and run the blade over my hand..."

"Dad, no!" I cried.

But I saw, with my own eyes, it did not cut him.

When he brought it closer to me and ran the plastic blade over my hand, Dad said, "You owe Mason an apology."

Still shaking, tears ran down my cheek as I tried to get the words out. "I'm sorry."

CHAPTER 18

My dad said he would wait downstairs and left us alone. Mason tried to hug me, but I pushed him away.

"Everything I've been through, and you do this to me!?"

"Do what to you?" Mason raised his voice. "I'm trying to be loving and understanding, but every time you throw it back in my face."

How could he say that? He didn't understand. But thinking about it, neither did I.

I was losing it when I screamed the words, "GET OUT! We're through for good!"

I didn't mean it, and I expected a different reaction, but I was in for a shock. Mason glared at me as he grabbed the duffel bag, searching each drawer until he found his clothes. He stuffed them into the bag, grabbed the knife I'd freaked over and made sure I noticed as he dropped it into the bag.

"A fake knife ruined our relationship... Good one, Em... Just great."

He got to the doorway, turned around and slammed a key down. "Your house key back."

His face was full of hurt. Why couldn't I just let him hug me...*oh God, what have I done?*

His footsteps went down the stairs and my dad said something I couldn't make out, and then the door slammed shut.

I heard that voice again. "Oh well...never mind... Now it's just you and me *forever*."

I was about to scream when my dad entered the room.

"Do you want to talk about it?"

I fell into his arms. "What have I done?" I whispered. "I need help, and I need Mason."

He held me. "Sweetheart, you accused him of planning something awful. You both need time to calm down. He looked devastated to be leaving. Emily, he loves you a lot."

That was it; I started to sob into my dad's chest.

Dad agreed to stay the night due to the circumstances, and it was nice with just the two of us, but I couldn't help but think of Mason.

"Emily, looking at your phone won't make it suddenly ring."

"Why hasn't he rung? I mean, I know I was a bitch, and yes, I can admit when I'm wrong."

My dad raised an eyebrow. "Stubborn is more the word. Are you having more of these dreams?" I glanced away, and he continued, "That means yes. Time to go to the doctor's."

I knew I had to be more forceful with the doctors, so I just agreed with my dad and tried to change the subject. "Have you seen Mum?"

"We're talking again, so we'll see. Before you ask any further questions, it's a start. Anyway—night, sweetheart, and see you in the morning."

* * *

As I lay in bed, I started to cry again. I picked up my mobile and rang Mason, but there was no answer. A text came through, but it wasn't from him: *Hey thought you should know Amy is throwing herself at Mason*. I bolted upright in bed. That bitch was after my Mason—she'd better keep her hands to herself. Then I remembered

I'd broken up with him and he was a free man. The tears came back.

A photo came through. Mason had his head down while holding a beer, and Amy was kissing him. David, his friend from work, had sent the texts and photo and one last message: *I don't know what went on but Mason is wasted. Amy is trying it on but he isn't interested.*

A smile crept onto my face, but then I heard the voice again. It was laughing at me.

"What do you want?" I shouted out, but there was no reply.

For a moment, there was silence, and then: "I have won and you have lost. Now let the games begin, and I promise, we will meet soon."

CHAPTER 19

I was looking out the window when my team leader approached me.

"Emily, are you forgetting something?"

"No, why?"

He looked pissed off. "You have been sitting in 'not ready' for fifteen minutes, and that is unacceptable."

I looked at the phone in front of me and quietly said, "Shit!" Then I glanced back at my team leader and shrugged my shoulders.

That was it—he kicked off. "Emily, your attendance to work and your quality of work is just not good enough. I think we need a chat, and this could lead to a disciplinary."

For a moment, I sat in shocked silence, and then, as the hurt of the comments settled in, demanded to see him in private. Once in a room, I firmly said, "I'm sorry my attendance is poor and my quality of work is not good enough, but I have stuff going on in my private life that needs my attention more than work." I wanted to break down, but I held my emotions back as I continued. "You have no right to call me out on the floor in front of the team and other people. I would hope that you would show concern, but I can see you can't do that for me."

"Emily, if I'm not told anything, how can I understand?"

"You want to know, then here it is: I'm trying to

see a doctor and I have accused my boyfriend of trying to hurt me and I broke up with him, so my world is falling apart. There. Now you know. Any questions?" I hurried to the door and had my hand on the handle when he said, "I'm sorry... Look, go home and get yourself sorted, then—and only then—come back."

I breathed in slowly and then turned to him. "Thank you, and sorry for raising my voice."

* * *

Outside Mason's place of work, David saw me.

"You look like crap." He stated the obvious.

I failed at a half-smile. "Is he in today?"

David shook his head. "He called in sick." I was shocked, and I think he sensed that. "He's lost without you, and just so you know, he told Amy to piss off."

I thanked David and took off to Mason's home. When I got there, I knocked on the door, but there was no answer. I started to bang on the door, but still there was no answer, so I reluctantly left.

When I got home, I understood how badly I had hurt Mason but felt powerless to fix things between us. My dad had popped around to see how I was doing. I told him that I'd tried to see Mason but there was no answer.

"Are you really surprised after the way you treated him?" he said.

I glanced away. "Not really, but I want to put things right, if I can."

"I understand, but you have to give this time..."

"But—"

"Emily, you've broken his trust and fixing that will take time. Now, did you get an earlier appointment with the doctor?"

I didn't want to talk about the doctors, I wanted to talk about Mason, but I answered, "Not yet, but while you're here, I'll try."

I rang them and was told that there was a space in two weeks rather than six, so I accepted it and told my dad.

After my dad left, I still tried to ring Mason, but there was no answer. I looked at the clock; it said eleven-thirty, so I tried to sleep. When I looked at the time again, it was three o'clock, and my eyes still felt heavy. Out of habit, I picked up my mobile. There was a missed call from Mason. He wanted to speak to me. I bolted upright in bed. I dialled his number, and when it connected I couldn't keep the smile from my face.

"Mason, I'm so, so sorry. Please can we talk face to face?"

"You think you can make everything alright."

Then I heard that evil laugh again. It wasn't Mason on the phone.

"Let the games begin," the voice said.

I screamed as I threw my phone across the room. In horror, I watched a figure pick up my phone and place it in my hand. I screamed again as I saw the knife. I watched in terror as it plunged into my chest over and over, hearing with every strike, "Isn't this fun?" followed by the cackling laugh.

CHAPTER 20

I knelt by the toilet, heaving into the bowl. The nightmares were getting worse. Mason wasn't talking to me, and I had no idea what was wrong with me. My mobile was ringing, but it was in the bedroom while I was stuck in the bathroom. I struggled back to the bedroom and saw I'd missed a call from my friend Laura.

When I called her back, she sounded worried. "You're still coming to the party tomorrow night?"

"The Halloween party—that's tomorrow?"

"Yes, and I'm freaking out. Please say you're still coming?"

I sat on the bed, feeling like crap. "I'll be there, but I'm coming on my own."

"Shit, I forgot you had a fight..." There was concern in Laura's voice.

"Laura, I broke up with him... I didn't mean to, but I lost my temper, and all I want is to be with him. I even bought a slutty witch outfit so he'd keep looking at me at this party, but now what's the point..." I trailed off before I started to cry again.

"Get that costume on, take a picture and send it to him with a comment saying, 'see what you are missing'. And when you do, make sure to wear a push-up bra so he comes running back."

Laura always knew what to say, and she was right. I got dressed up, took the photo and pressed send on the phone with the message, 'please come back and I'm sorry.'

There was a knock at my door. I hurried down the stairs to answer it in case it was Mason, but even if he had seen the picture, he couldn't have got here this quickly. I was shocked to see my brother, Mark, standing at the door with a suitcase.

"Hi, Em. I'm between houses—can I stay with you?"

I stepped aside. "Why don't you stay with your girlfriend?" I asked.

He looked at me and said smugly, "If she answered the door dressed like that, then we'd still be together… I didn't interrupt you and Mason, you know…doing it, did I?"

I slammed the door shut. "I wish, but we've broken up."

He looked at me in shock. "What the fuck, Em? You guys are awesome together—plus he and I get on."

Suddenly, I noticed my brother's brown hair was slightly longer and looked dirty. Come to think of it, he looked scruffy, which wasn't him. I mean, we all have down days, but even though he dressed mostly in casual wear, Mark always took pride in his appearance. I decided not to say anything and carry on with our conversation.

We sat down, and I explained what had happened.

"Have you tried to talk to him?"

I shook my head. "I've called at his house, and I've taken a picture dressed like this, but nothing."

Mark stood up and said, "I'll see you shortly, and I'll be bringing Mason with me."

"Mark, you can't get involved," I shouted after him, but it was too late—he had left my house.

* * *

Mark

I was going to get Mason to listen to me. I wanted to see my sister happy again.

"Fucking open the door, Mason. If you don't, I'll just force my way in."

Finally, the door opened and, before Mason could say anything, I barged my way past. I sat in a chair in the living room and when Mason finally came in, he looked like crap.

"So, what's the deal with you and my sister?"

He finished his can and threw it across the room in a temper. "She accused me of trying to kill her and told me we are through."

"Come on, Mase... We both know that Em didn't mean it."

"You weren't there, Mark!" Mason yelled at the top of his voice. "Something is going on—she's hiding stuff from me, then she thinks I would hurt her but I would never..." He opened another can. "I'd never... I love her. The day before she broke my heart, I was looking at rings..."

"Wow... Are you saying what I think you're saying?"

Mason threw himself on the sofa and replied quietly, "Yes I am... Marriage."

I was stunned. "Then come with me and sort things out."

"She will only push me away again."

"Have you checked your phone?"

"No, why?"

"Check it."

Mason picked up his phone and checked his messages. A smile crept across his face. "I have things to do. I'll see you soon."

I nodded and, as I walked out the door, I shouted back, "Have a shower too—you stink."

* * *

I ran to my brother when he walked in. "Where's Mason?"

"He's at home feeling sorry for himself. Just give him time."

I nodded. It was a relief to hear that. "Tell me why you and your girlfriend broke up."

He put his arm around me and said, "Well, it all started…"

This was going to be a long night.

CHAPTER 21

I'd just grabbed my keys when Mark shouted down the stairs.

"Em, I couldn't tag along to that party you're going to, could I?"

I looked up the stairs at my brother and sighed. "I guess it would be alright, but no hitting on my friends."

He laughed. "Give me the list and I'll avoid them, scout's honour."

I glared at him. "You were never in the scouts, only cubs. Just behave, OK?"

"Fine, I won't have sex tonight…happy?"

I smiled at his grumpy look. "Ecstatic."

Then I quickly left to help Laura.

* * *

When I got there, Laura dragged me straight into the kitchen.

"Look at all these boxes," she said.

"What's in the boxes?" I asked.

Laura raised an eyebrow as if I had said something weird. "Halloween decorations, and the party's in a few hours and, as you can see, there are no decorations up… Help."

"Laura, take a seat and breathe. Everything will be OK and all the decorations will be up and ready in time for the party."

She looked at me. "Thank you—I don't know what I'd have done without you."

I checked my phone. Mason hadn't called me.

"Put that damn phone away," Laura said firmly.

I looked at her in disbelief, but she was right—I needed a distraction and helping with this party was it.

We decided that Laura would start on the decorations and I'd start on the food. I was getting everything prepared when I heard a cough from behind and, when I looked, a guy was leaning against the kitchen door.

He smiled at me. "I'm Ben, Laura's brother."

He was tall and slim, and even through his T-shirt, I could tell he had muscles. However, I thought back to Mason who—in my opinion— had a good body and well-defined muscles, but maybe I was biased.

My cheeks were going bright red and I didn't know why.

"Hi, Ben—I'm Emily," I replied quickly.

"Hi, Emily. You need a hand? Because to be honest, I'd rather be in here than out there with my sister, who is flapping."

I had to laugh because it was true—Laura was in a state. "I guess you can help. I take it you can make sandwiches?"

He laughed. "I think I can stretch to making sandwiches."

After that, we got on with making the food. Lots of noise was coming from the living room, and then suddenly Laura shouted.

"I better see what she wants before she hurts herself," Ben said to me.

I nodded in agreement as Ben left to help Laura while I got on with the remaining food. Once I'd finished the last of it, I looked at my phone— still nothing. I checked if he'd read the text with the picture. He had, but there was no reply. The realisation hit that we were really over and I burst into tears.

Laura must have heard. She walked in and gave me a hug.

"He's an idiot, hon."

I spoke through my tears. "He saw the picture, and nothing... It's really over."

"Look at me, Em." As I looked her in the eye, she continued, "If that didn't get his attention, then he's an ass."

"Shouldn't I ring him? I mean, I have to try something."

Laura sighed. "I really don't think there's anything else you can do. I mean, you've tried everything. I hate saying this, but think of this party as a fresh start... A new beginning to a new you and your future."

"But I want the future I had."

Although... she was right. I'd tried everything and nothing had worked—not even my brother had got Mason to the house to talk. I had well and truly fucked this relationship up.

"Now, let's get ready for this party."

I wiped my tears away and gave a half-hearted attempt at a smile. "OK, let's get ready."

I went to go through to the living room, but Laura held me back. "Not that way. I want it to be a surprise for everyone. If we go through this door, we can get to the stairs that way and get ready."

I shook my head and laughed slightly. "I have to say it, Laura—you are weird."

"I try my best."

When I'd finished putting on the last of my makeup, Laura said, "Wow, if there are any guys at this party tonight—which there will be—they won't be able to take their eyes off you. You look hot."

CHAPTER 22

When the doorbell went, Laura turned into a big kid.

"Oh my god!" she said. "People are actually here... People came!"

I had to laugh as she continued to fuss. "Just go downstairs and answer the door."

She stopped in her tracks. "Yes, you're right. Are you coming?"

"I'll be there in a minute; I just have to use the bathroom."

After Laura had disappeared, I sat on the bed and took a moment to myself. I could hear lots of people's voices, so I checked my face in the mirror one more time and headed downstairs. As I was starting down the stairs and saw people in costumes, I started to feel sick. I didn't know why, but suddenly a rush of fear swept over me. It must have just been to do with all the issues of the past few weeks—breaking up with Mason had hit me hard. However, I decided to put it at the back of my mind and enjoy the party.

When I entered the living room, I looked around at all the decorations Laura had done—cobwebs over the window, a spider on the ceiling and a pumpkin over the fireplace. The door to the kitchen had black all around it that she had created out of bin bags, and above the door it said, 'The Horror Grotto Here'. When I approached the kitchen door and saw inside, that had also been decorated—her brother must have done last-minute decorating while we were upstairs.

As I turned back to head towards the hallway with the front door, my head started to spin. Everyone was in costume, and most of them had masks on. I was starting to sweat and to panic— there was no way out. I was terrified and all I knew was that I was frightened and I wanted out. I kept looking for an escape, but everywhere I looked, people were trying to talk to me. I quickly ran towards the hallway and back up the stairs and locked myself in the bathroom.

While the tears ran down my face, I rocked back and forth, and then I heard, "Welcome to my games. Have you figured it out yet?"

I screamed at the top of my voice, "Fuck off and leave me alone!"

I was shaking, and I needed to get out of this house and home. I went to get my phone so I could get help, but because of this stupid costume, I'd left my mobile in Laura's room. I tried to get up, but my legs wouldn't let me. I felt vulnerable and my mind raced all over the place. I needed my phone, but how was that going to happen with me in this state?

I tried to pull myself up again, and this time it worked, but I was very unstable on my feet. When I slowly opened the door, people were coming up and down the stairs. I shut the door again. I hugged myself as I slid down the door. I curled up into a ball, hoping this would all end soon.

Suddenly there was a loud bang on the door and a voice said, "Fucking hurry up! I need a piss."

I couldn't answer. As I kept an eye on the door, I rocked back and forth. The voice shouted again—I didn't register what was said—and then there was a knock on the door.

"Who's in there?"

I recognised that voice—it was Laura.

Trembling, I tried to speak, but I had no voice. I struggled to open the door, and when I did, Laura walked in. She saw me and gasped.

"Em, what happened?"

I struggled to get a sentence out, and she said, "Your brother, Mark, is here. Do you want me to get him?"

I nodded, and she hurried to find him. Within a few minutes, she was back, a masked man at her side. I screamed, scrambling backwards, but my back was already against the wall.

The mask was removed and I saw it was Mark. "Emily, it's me. You know, your annoying brother."

My eyes stayed focused on the mask. Mark quickly picked it up and put it outside the door. Then he looked at me.

"Emily, calm down and talk to me."

Through the fear and tears, I begged, "Get me out. Please."

"You want to go home?"

I nodded and all I remember was Mark saying, "I'm taking you home."

CHAPTER 23

The following morning, thinking about the night before felt weird. The memory was foggy and surreal, like it hadn't really happened, but I knew deep down it had. The night's experience had left me numb and shaken.

I was deep in thought when I heard the front door. I jumped, but I heard Mark's voice and started to calm down.

"Sis, it's me." He poked his head around the door. "You were sleeping, so I took your house keys rather than wake you."

I smiled. "You can come into the kitchen."

Mark came in. "How are you this morning?" he asked.

I took a sip of my tea. "Last night felt so surreal; I just don't get it."

Mark started to respond but, suddenly, my mind was miles away as I started having flashbacks.

Waking up in the middle of the night, I was frightened. The darkness scared me; sweat poured from my body, which shook as I got out of bed. I was terrified that something was coming to get me. I ran across the hall to the living room to see if my parents were still awake. They weren't there, but the television was left on. I couldn't take my eyes off the screen as a masked man came through the door, slicing the person in front of him from the stomach upwards as if he were a piece of meat. The masked person continued through the house to find the next poor unfortunate soul.

I ran from the room, screaming. I was now terrified beyond my comprehension. The masked man was coming for me, but where could I hide? Wait—there was no escape from my hell.

My parents came from their bedroom, wondering what was wrong. I told them a horrible man was coming and would not stop till he sliced me too.

They told me it was a film and nothing to be concerned about. The masked man was not out to get me—it was just acting and nothing to be afraid of. I took this at face value and thought nothing more about it. Until last night, that was.

I felt sick, but why hadn't I seen this before? Maybe I had been in denial—I don't know—but I hoped I would have answers soon so I could stop worrying about all this and get back to a normal life, whatever that meant for me.

"Earth to Sis," Mark said. "Are you listening to me?"

Suddenly, I snapped back to the present. "Sorry, Mark, I was miles away. What did you say?"

Mark looked pissed at me. "I was telling you about my new job, and that I have a date tonight."

I looked at him and raised my eyebrow. "Not a girl from last night's party that I have no good memory of?"

"I know—I know that I said I'd behave, but she was hot and I couldn't help myself, and then you happened... Anyway, she's meeting me tonight."

I looked at him with disbelief, but after what had happened and how he'd helped me, I responded, "I hope you have a good time."

My mobile beeped at me with a text from Laura: *Hope u r ok. Let me know u r ok.*

I texted back: *Hi, I'm still shaken but better than last night, speak soon x.*

"Mark, you haven't told Mum or Dad about last night?" I said.

"No—I thought I'd leave that up to you."

I left Mark in the kitchen, stuffing himself with food. I was sat in the living room, just staring into space, when I heard, "I see you haven't forgotten about me."

I jumped up and looked around the room, but there was no one there. Then that laugh came.

"Good—I'm glad you still remember. I'll always be here."

I broke down in tears as I sat back down. Mark's music was on loud in the kitchen, so he couldn't hear me. Maybe being off work was getting to me. I knew my team leader had said to sort myself out, but I needed normality. Time away from the house and being back at work might be just what I needed.

I called someone in Human Resources and asked them to let my team leader know that I would be returning to work tomorrow. I was unsure about going back to work, but I also felt that it was the right thing to do.

* * *

I was heading towards town when I saw a shadowy figure in the distance. I glanced down; the figure was holding a knife. I changed direction, but the figure was in front of me, still in the distance. I quickened my pace and changed direction again. This time, the figure was closer than before, just staring at me. Still, I could not see their face. Fear gripped me as I walked another way, but each time, the figure was still in front of me.

Suddenly, a car beeped its horn. When I looked

up, I realised I was in the middle of the road and was almost run over. I froze with panic.

The driver got out and shouted, "Emily, are you trying to get killed?"

It was Mason.

CHAPTER 24

Mason told, not asked, me to get in the car, and he took me back to his place. Once the front door closed, Mason said, "Do you want a drink?"

I looked at him. "Yes, thank you," I replied softly.

"Go into the living room and I'll be there in a few moments."

As I walked into the living room, I noticed how messy it was, but sat on the sofa. Moments later, Mason came in with a cup of tea and sat next to me.

"Aren't you having a drink?"

His expression was neutral and I couldn't tell what was on his mind, but I could guess. It was probably everything I'd said and done to him.

"I'm not thirsty, but I was on my way to see you because I think we need to talk." I stared at my tea and listened as he continued, "I heard what happened last night; do you want to talk about it?"

What? No "You fucking bitch, accusing me of trying to kill you"?

I looked at him, and calmly said, "Mason, I'm so sorry about—" but he interrupted me.

"You accused me of trying to kill you and then told me we are through…why?"

The truth was I couldn't give a good answer to that. He was right.

"I don't know why, but I didn't want to break up with you. You were right—I should have been upfront about everything."

Mason looked at me for a moment. "I thought about staying away, but I realised I don't want to stay away. I should—you can't accuse me of things I haven't done, and you need to be honest with me. Now, tell me about last night."

I started to explain the previous night to him. He listened intently as I told him, even when at some points of my story I cried, sounded scared and started to shake. Once I was done, he stayed silent for a moment and then pulled me in for a hug.

"Have you got the appointment with the doctor yet?" he asked quietly.

I pulled away and looked at him. "No. I mean, I have one in two weeks' time, if that counts."

He took my hand and smiled. "I'll come with you, if you don't mind."

"It's nice of you," I said nervously, smiling back, "but I treated you badly, and we aren't together anymore."

"Did you understand what I said earlier, Em?" I looked puzzled, and he added, "When I said I should stay away but I can't, it meant that I want us to still be together. I stormed out very angry and upset, but I have no intention of that stubborn streak of yours letting a good relationship go, so I guess you're still stuck with me."

I leaped over to him, almost knocking him over, and hugged him tightly as tears started down my face again.

"I love you so much," I whispered. "I know it's probably the wrong time, but if the offer is still there, then I want us to move in together."

Mason pulled away and looked at me, smiling. "I'd love that, too. Do you want me to stay today?"

I nodded with a smile.

It was going to be a long road for us, but he

was willing to still be there after the shit I threw his way, and that said a lot. It would be worth it in the end.

"Last night, do you know what caused it?" Mason asked suddenly.

I glared at him. "I'm not sure, but when I saw everyone dressed up, I know it scared me enough that I hid in Laura's bathroom. I just hope the doctor can give me the answers I need."

"Let's hope so. By the way, the picture you sent in the witch's costume was very sexy."

I blushed and quickly asked, "What do you think the doctor will say about what's happened?"

"Honestly, I don't know. I've never known anyone like you before. Before you say anything—I don't mean it in a bad way. I just don't know the answer."

I had my suspicions, but I would have to wait until I saw the doctor to have it all confirmed. I did wonder, however, if the doctor would think I was being silly—or worse, making it all up. I knew I was telling the truth and, after last night, I knew it wasn't all in my head. Now all I had to do was convince the doctor so that I would know once and for all that I wasn't crazy.

CHAPTER 25

I was in the reception area, waiting for a team leader to do my return to work, for what felt like hours before one finally showed up.

"Hi, Emily," he said as we sat down. "Are you OK to return to work?"

I glanced at him and replied, "Yes."

"Can I ask the reason for the absence from work?"

"Stress!"

He wrote it down on the paperwork. "Have you seen the doctor?"

"I have an appointment in two weeks, but I haven't seen anyone yet. I feel better now."

He nodded, filled in a few lines on the form and handed it to me to read and sign. I quickly read the document, and it said exactly what we had discussed. I signed it and gave it back.

"If your percentage is over three percent, then you will have another meeting with your team leader."

Oh great—the percentage thing again. That was all they cared about, how much time you were away from work.

I nodded that I understood and made my way to my desk. Before my shift started, I disappeared to the drinks machine and, when I came back, some of the team had arrived. They said morning, and most asked if I was feeling better.

"You're back just in time," Scott said. "We're decorating our area today."

I nodded and asked, "Why?"

He looked at me as if I'd been on another planet. "It's October, so we're decorating the area for Halloween."

My heart stopped as I processed the information. "Great," I said evenly, then turned to my desk to set up the computer for the work day ahead.

Why had Laura's party been so early? Oh right—she was going to another Halloween event. That must have been it.

I checked the time, logged in and started to take calls. About twenty minutes later, my team leader came beside me.

"After this call, go into 'not ready', as we're having a team meeting."

Oh great, another meeting. I smiled and nodded that I had received the message.

Five minutes later, I finished the call and sat with the other team members. Once everyone was present, my team leader started the meeting. "Now we're all here, just a few business points to go through, and then we can get to the fun stuff."

Some of the team took the opportunity to talk with each other and have a laugh, and to be honest, I couldn't blame them. Half the time it felt like they were cracking the whip to get more out of us. The team leader cleared his throat loudly to get everyone's attention.

After a while, he said, "Now that's all over, as I said earlier, time for the fun stuff. As you all know, Halloween is just around the corner, and it's that time again to decorate our area. Some of you have brought in your own decorations, but we were also given a small budget and I bought some last night. We're lucky to have half an hour off the phones to decorate, so let's get started."

Great—just what I needed. I tried to sit back at my desk, but my team leader caught me. "Come on—help."

"Fine."

I held open the bin bags while the others took the decorations out and started putting them up. Someone put cobwebs around my desk, and I wasn't happy because all I could think of was spiders and I hated spiders, but I gritted my teeth and just smiled back.

When our area was done, it looked how you would expect—dark and dingy. By the end of the day a few more teams had put up the decorations. After the other night, I just wasn't in the mood, but hopefully, the closer Halloween got, I would get into the spirit of it and start having fun.

Laura caught me on the way out as we were leaving work. "How are you now?"

I smiled. "Doing much better, and sorry."

"Don't be sorry, I'm just glad you're OK, and I'm glad you're back in work. Are you doing anything this weekend?"

"Don't know yet, because Mason and I are talking again."

Laura had a smirk on her face. "I told you sending a picture in that costume would work."

But before I could reply, she disappeared.

CHAPTER 26

As I walked home from the train station, I thought about Mason and me. Even though he had stayed the night, after what I'd put him through the other week I'd suggested that we stay in separate rooms. He'd agreed and stayed on the sofa because Mark was in the spare room. I still felt bad for accusing him of trying to kill me. I couldn't understand why, but deep down, I knew Mason would never hurt me.

When I got home, there was a girl in my kitchen I didn't know.

"Hi," I said. "And you are?"

She turned around. She was wearing my shirt with no bottoms on, her long legs on show. She was slim, and no strand of her long brunette hair was out of place. Listen to me...I didn't even know her, and yet I was sounding jealous.

"I'm Lisa, and you must be Emily."

Mason walked in and asked if I wanted a drink. He smiled at Lisa, and all I could feel was my anger building.

"Who's Lisa?" I asked him as calmly as possible.

Mason burst into a smile. "Are you jealous?"

I was about to blow up at him when she interrupted. "I'd better get back to Mark before he wonders where I am. It was nice to meet you, Emily."

When she left, Mason started to laugh. "You thought she and I... Not even my type. And you think I'd bring her here to your place, when I have a place of my own? Mark let me in and introduced Lisa. I think he's seeing her."

I threw a tea towel at him. "You let me think that you two were together... You idiot."

Mason grabbed my waist. "No, you thought that all by yourself."

I hit his arm as he continued to smile at me. "And Mark doesn't do girlfriends...well, not long term anyway. But he brought her here, to my house... Wait till I see him."

"Let him have fun."

I glared at Mason before asking, "Why are you here?"

He kissed me. "Would you like to go to dinner?"

I smiled. "I'd love that, but I'll need to get changed first. I won't be long."

I quickly ran up the stairs and was looking in the wardrobe at what I could wear when I heard, "I'm still here, remember."

Panic suddenly washed over me. I tried to stay calm. "Go away and leave me alone."

"You forget—I'll always be with you, and I'm not going anywhere."

My body reacted to the voice as panic started to creep in. Trying to breathe and stay calm, I carried on looking at my clothes when there was a rattle at my window.

"Oh God, no. Please just let it be the wind or something like that."

I went over and nothing was there. When I looked out onto the street, the shadowy figure was there again, just looking at me with the knife in his hand.

"Don't fight it," said the voice. "If you don't, it will be all over soon."

I screamed, backed away from the window

and fell onto the bed. I was losing my mind. That had to be the answer, right?

Mark and Mason both barged into my room and firmly asked in unison, "What's wrong?"

I looked at them both, almost in tears. "Someone is outside, holding a knife, and I heard a voice tell me to accept my fate."

Mason held me while Mark looked out of the window.

"Sis," he said, "there's no one there."

"There was someone there—I saw them," I screamed at my brother.

Mark knelt down and looked me in the eye. "Sis, I believe you, but no one is there now." He looked up at the doorway and said, "Sorry, I'll be there now."

Lisa responded to him, but I couldn't hear her clearly, and then he turned his attention back to me. We looked at each other, and he asked, "Are you OK?"

I wiped my tears while I held onto Mason and replied through the sniffles. "I'll be OK."

Mark glanced at Mason and then left us alone. Mason hadn't said anything, just held me close.

"Do you want to talk about it?" he asked.

I didn't pull away, just stayed where I was. "I saw a figure outside the window, I swear…"

"I believe you, but you need to calm down and take slow breaths."

I tried to follow his advice, but it was very hard. All I knew was that what I'd seen was real. No one would be able to convince me any differently.

CHAPTER 27

After the blur of the last couple of weeks, I was determined not to let things get to me. That's what I kept telling myself, anyway.

I got into work early and was greeted with our dark scenes. Everywhere I turned in the office, there was some sort of Halloween decoration. It made my stomach want to turn. I'd never been overly keen on this holiday, but I tried to not let it bother me.

When the rest of my team got in, they asked why I hadn't dressed up. I let them know I'd forgotten about dressing up and had just come in my normal officewear. Some of them looked puzzled, but we all settled in to do our job.

An hour later, more of our team came in, fully dressed up in costumes with masks. I couldn't look at them for long and struggled to settle and focus on my work. One member of my team started to complain that he couldn't do his job with his mask on, so he took it off and put it to the side, where I was sitting. I started to move over towards the window because, out of the corner of my eye, I could see the mask and was starting to feel terrified.

I put myself into 'not ready' and went towards the bathroom. I passed more people dressed up in full costumes and some wearing no costume, just a mask, and I started to feel sick. Once I got to the bathroom, I splashed water on my face in case that would help me calm down, but nothing was working. Every time the bathroom door opened, I panicked in case it was somebody in costume. I was now in full panic mode—my anxiety levels were horrible, and I started to cry out of fear. This was all made worse by the fact that I did not know what was going on, but one thing I did understand was I really needed to see the doctor about what was happening to me, and soon.

Eventually, I tried to leave the bathroom, but when I saw more costumes walking around with the surroundings all dark and gloomy, I started to panic again and ran back inside. At this point, I was out of control, shaking, crying and panicking.

A woman who had come into the bathroom was kind enough to ask if I was OK and said that she would get someone to come in and see me. I paced in the bathroom and just couldn't face going back in the office area but, at this point, I had no choice. A team leader came into the bathroom and asked what was going on.

"I'm not sure," I replied, "but all I know is... the decorations and people... walking in costumes... masks. I feel... I don't know. Why is this happening?"

They looked at me in shock, but said, "Just go to your car, and I'll get someone to bring your things, and you can go home for today."

"I didn't bring my car today; I came by train."

"If you just wait outside then. As I said, I'll get someone to bring your things out to you."

I gave a half smile and rushed outside into the fresh air. It felt like taking my first breath after years of suffocation. As I waited outside, I called Mason. Shocked by the terror in my voice, he told me not to move and that he would pick me up in fifteen minutes. During that short time before he came and got me, I must have smoked half a pack of cigarettes, trying my best to calm down.

When Mason pulled up, I just got in the car and said, "Drive."

I didn't even bother with a 'Hi, how was your day?'

He saw by my expression that I wasn't in a good way and said, "I contacted the doctors, and you're going now."

"What?!" I yelled

"Whatever this is has gone on long enough. When I was firm with the receptionist, she said there was an appointment available in an hour, so I'm taking you there now."

I wanted to be mad with him, but even I knew I had to see the doctor and quickly.

As he drove me, the rest of the car journey was spent in silence as I tried to work out how to explain what was going on to the doctors.

CHAPTER 28

When my name was called, I followed the doctor into the room and took a seat. She smiled at me.

"Emily, what can I help you with?" she asked.

I looked at Mason, sitting by me, and then back at Dr Lane. I rubbed my hands together due to nerves and then, taking a deep breath, I explained what was going on:

"You might think I'm mad, but it started a while back with nightmares of a figure chasing me. I never see their face, but the situations are always different. Sometimes I wake up frightened and in fear. I also think I see the figure when I'm awake, but it could just be my imagination. Then I walked past shops in town with masks on display and started to panic, so ran past the shops as quickly as possible. The most recent events have been when I went to a Halloween party and locked myself in the bathroom because people were in costumes and masks and I freaked out. I started sweating, felt an overwhelming sense of fear and like I was going to be sick. I thought they were coming to get me, and the same thing happened today when I was at work, because they decorated the office for Halloween and people dressed up. Am I mad?"

Dr Lane looked at me. "Emily, you aren't mad," she said. "What you are describing is a phobia."

My head spun at the word. "A phobia?"

"It is a rare phobia and, by the sound of it, you have two phobias: the Halloween phobia is known as Samhainophobia, and the one for the masks is known as Maskaphobia. In your case, it sounds like the mask one refers to the horror genre."

I looked at her carefully and thought it over before answering, "It makes sense, but I've never been like this before. So why now?"

"It could be the decorations in an area and the people dressed up all at the same time triggered it, and now it has made you more aware of it."

"I knew I was never overly keen on Halloween, but I never thought this."

Suddenly, Mason asked, "Is there a cure?"

The doctor looked at him and answered, "You can get help, and I will ask Emily to be put forward for counselling, and I hope they can help you further."

"So this will go away?" I asked her quickly.

"With the right help, you should be able to manage the phobia, and it may be possible to cure it, but there are no guarantees."

"Yes—if you could get me counselling so I can get rid of this then that would be great. How long will I have to wait?"

"We have a counsellor on site, so possibly six to eight weeks."

* * *

It was as if a weight had been lifted as I left the doctor's. When I got home, Mason looked up what I'd been told.

"Shit, the phobias really exist," he said to me in shock.

"The doctor wouldn't lie about something like that." There was anger in my voice. "I'm in shock, just like you, but this does explain a lot."

"She didn't say about the voices you've been hearing."

Now he thought I was a mental case. We had an answer, so why couldn't he just be grateful for that? I needed space, so I left the room and went to the kitchen, but Mason followed me.

"Look, I'm sorry, but you have to admit it's a lot to take in. I never thought it could be that."

"It is a lot to process, but I'm going to be getting help. Just because she didn't mention the voices doesn't mean I'm mental…"

"Now, Em, I never said you were mental…"

"But you thought it…"

"No. But I was surprised she didn't talk about the voices as well."

Trying to stay calm, I replied, "Have you ever thought the reason why is because it's all connected and, if I go to the counselling, then it will all get sorted?"

He looked at me. "Sorry. And yes—you could be right."

Now I knew the truth, I realised that some of the dreams had been reality for me, and this dislike of Halloween had started back when I was a child.

CHAPTER 29

I needed time alone, so Mason agreed to go home that night. I mean, I wasn't totally alone— my brother and his new flavour-of-the-month girlfriend were in the spare room. I took a long soak in the bath, which helped me unwind and relax. Then I climbed into bed and curled up with a book, which I hadn't done in a long time.

I must've fallen asleep, because when I woke up, sweat was pouring from me. I couldn't understand why, but an overwhelming sense of fear swept over me. I looked across the bed. In front of my dressing table was a shadowy figure, wearing what appeared to be a white top. I tried to close my eyes tightly and pretend I hadn't seen anything, but this didn't calm me down. I bolted upright and switched the light on. When I forced myself to look back over to the dressing table, nothing was there.

When I got up the following morning, I felt like I'd barely slept. I replayed the night's events in my head. I knew I had been under a lot of stress lately, wanting to know what was going on and why, but I thought that having some explanation from the doctor meant I could relax more. Obviously, that was not to be the case.

I was still thinking about the night before when the doorbell went. I went to answer it, but my brother got there first. He let Mason in and said, "Morning, mate."

"Morning. How are things with you?"

Mark gave a cocky smile. All I wanted to do was throw up because I knew my brother too well, but so did Mason.

"That's how things went...lucky you." Mason looked at me, and I must've given him a frown or something because he said, "Don't look at me like that—at the end of the day, all men want sex."

I quickly changed the subject. "So what brings you around this morning?"

"I know you wanted to be on your own last night, but I thought I'd come round for breakfast."

I rolled my eyes. "You mean there was nothing in your fridge or cupboards, so you thought you'd come here!"

With a laugh, he replied, "You know me so well."

I began to cook breakfast, and the image from last night popped into my head again. As I thought about it more and more, I decided I needed to keep Mason up to date with what was going on.

I made us a cup of coffee, and I told him, "I had another dream." He looked at me intently as if he was waiting for more, so I carried on. "I woke up last night, and this figure...well, I think it was a figure...was in front of my dressing table with what appeared to be a white top on. The top looked like it belonged to a female, but to be honest, I'm not sure if what I saw was real or if I was imagining it. Maybe all the stress I've been under caused this, but who knows... I know—sounds crazy, right?"

As I tried to get all this out quickly, Mason's expression was even and unreadable. He just listened and sipped his coffee. I'd expected him to interrupt me or say something, but he didn't.

It was quiet for a few moments, and then

Mason said calmly, "This could be down to many things, and one of them could be what you said—stress being a major factor. I think you should write all this down so when you see the counsellor, you can tell them, and hopefully they can help you to understand what's going on."

I have to admit, his reaction puzzled me, because I'd expected him to not believe me or to dismiss it...in fact, I'm not even sure what I had expected, but that reaction was definitely a welcome change.

I smiled at him. "Hopefully it's just the stress that I've been under that's causing all this, but I'm baffled because this is something new..."

"Em, you will be fine, but you just have to make sure you tell the counsellor everything so that they get the full picture and can help you." He grabbed my hand and, with a reassuring smile, squeezed it tightly. "Now, we better serve up the breakfast before it gets burned."

CHAPTER 30

After we finished breakfast, Mark appeared.

"You had cooked breakfast and didn't cook me any…"

"No, I didn't, because you don't live here… Well, not permanently. And besides, you can cook your own food."

Mark wasn't impressed. Before he could open his mouth, I continued, "You can always move back in with Mum and ask her to cook."

He made a face at the idea. "Move in with Mum…no way. Not happening. She'd grill me about my life, especially my love life. I'll get, 'Mark, why haven't you made me a grandmother yet?' and 'When are you going to settle down?' Sis, you know what she's like, and I can't deal with the full-on Mum mode that she'd go into."

I had to admit he was right—Mum was full-on. I mean, we loved our mum, but there were times that I could have strangled her because of her interrogations…sometimes.

"Don't 'Sis' me. I know you're right about Mum, but at the same time, I'm not the maid, the cook or anything else you can think of. I mean, you bring this new girl into my house…"

"Lisa…"

"Whatever… She's staying here, but you didn't ask me—"

"Didn't think I'd have to, *Mum*."

Suddenly I saw red. "What did you just say?"

Mark stood his ground and spat back, "You

know, you used to be fun…you know, a chilled-out sister, and now you think you can tell me what to do—"

Mason got between us. "You're arguing over breakfast and who cooks it. Come on, both of you—snap out of it." Then he faced Mark. "You know Em has been dealing with shit."

"Look, just because you want to mar…" Mark quickly stopped what he was saying, and Mason glared at him. "What I mean is that you *would* take her side, but she's the one being snappy and I just reacted to it."

I butted in before Mason could speak. "One—I'm not snappy, but I've been under pressure, and second of all…what were you going to say before you cut off!?" There it was, that look between my brother and boyfriend, and I didn't like it. "OK, are you both up to something that I should know about?"

They both looked at me and said in unison, "Would we ever—"

"Yes, you would."

Then Mark said, "OK, yes, there was that time, but that was like…ages ago."

I narrowed my eyes. "You're a bad influence on each other."

Whatever they were up to, I wasn't going to get a straight answer out of either of them.

* * *

Mason

I waited till Em left the room and said in a low but firm tone, "You fucking dick…"

"Sorry, but Emily was winding me up."

I closed the gap between us. "What I said was

in confidence and was not to be repeated. I love your sister, but I choose when and where and *how* she finds out…understand?"

"Boy, you do have it bad for my sister. That is why I stopped."

I nudged Mark as I walked by. "Just keep your mouth shut."

* * *

Emily

Suddenly, my brother's voice shouted through the house, "I'm not cleaning up as I didn't eat or cook the breakfast."

"I'm doing them now," I shouted back as I walked from the living room.

When I got to the kitchen, it was empty. I started loading the dishwasher and heard, "There is no escape… Did you like my friend?"

I spun around, but there was no one there.

"Piss off and leave me alone," I muttered through gritted teeth.

"Can't do that. As I told you, you are stuck with me."

I suddenly felt sick and tried to control my breathing, but the voice kept taunting me.

"You think that will help? Go on, keep trying, but you and I both know it is a futile exercise as I'll still be here."

I had a plate in my hand and, before I knew it, I'd thrown it across the kitchen. When I looked at the floor, it was in tiny pieces.

"Am I getting to you?" The laugh radiated around the room. "I know I'm pushing your buttons. Now, let's see if you have better aim and can hit me."

The voice was goading me, and I took the bait. As I threw another plate, it narrowly missed Mason, who was walking back into the kitchen.

Looking really shocked, he shouted, "What the hell is going on?"

CHAPTER 31

I tried to shrug it off and started to clean up the mess, but Mason grabbed my arm.

"Em, what's going on?"

I looked up and met his eyes. They showed concern. Seeing that, I reluctantly answered, "I heard the voice again, and it was taunting me…"

He loosened his grip slightly. "Em, the voice isn't real, so ignore it."

I started to clean again. "Look, the voice is real to me, and I know what you're trying to say, but try and see it from my point of view. Please."

"I'm not trying to put you down, all I'm trying to say is whatever this is, you need to ignore it."

"You make it sound so easy… I just wish it was."

As I put the last of the plate in the bin, my emotions were all over the place. I knew Mason was trying to help, but the way he was coming across it was as if he did not understand. To be honest, though, how could he? He didn't have any of these horrible feelings and doubts that I had about what the doctor called a phobia.

Mason must have picked up on my concerns because his arms wrapped around my waist as he kissed my neck softly. "I know I don't have any idea how you are feeling, but I am trying to understand."

I turned my head slightly, kissing him. "I know you are. It's just...every time I talk to you, the face you give me says I'm talking crap and I'm going nuts." I pulled away and faced him.

"Now, Em, we both know you're already nuts—that's what I love about you—but this phobia the doctor says you have is just strange, so I'm trying to get my head around it… That's all."

The front door opened and I heard, "See you later, Sis."

Mason looked at me and said, "I need to get some clothes from my place, as I'll stay here tonight if that's OK with you?"

I nodded with a smile. "That would be nice."

"Do you want to come with me?"

"Thanks for the offer, but I have a few things to do here."

"See you shortly," he said, and kissed me on the cheek. Even though we'd started talking again, we still hadn't talked about moving, but it was still early days.

I went to my bedroom to change the sheets on my bed. As I started to strip the bed, I felt the silence in the house and I was very aware I was on my own. As I continued, a door creaked downstairs. I ignored it, but then I heard it again. Suddenly, I froze. More aware, I looked at the door. Nothing.

I continued making my bed and the door downstairs creaked for a third time. I couldn't leave it. I dropped the sheets and rushed to the door to look. I leaned over the banister, but nothing was there.

I returned to what I'd been doing, but my anxiety levels were already up to maximum. Suddenly aware of my surroundings, I kept looking at the door, expecting that man with the knife to appear from my dreams and kill me. I had to flee, get away from this overwhelming sense of doom.

I quickly ran downstairs and out the front door. I had only been there a few minutes when

Mason pulled up in his car. He took one look at me and I burst into tears. This was the first time he'd stayed silent as he held me and walked me back into the house.

I explained what had happened since he'd gone to his place.

"That's it," he said. "I know the doctor is putting you for counselling, but it needs to happen sooner."

He called the surgery but put me on the phone briefly to get authorisation to discuss my health. He was very firm with them. When he came off the phone, he told me that they were still waiting to hear from the hospital about the counselling, but the doctor's surgery had a counsellor on site that could see me next week. I was pleased I was starting to get somewhere, but for now I was in a mess.

I was still shaking when Mason asked, "Do you want help finishing the bed?"

I nodded, but fear paralysed me at the foot of the stairs, looking up.

I turned away and headed back to the living room.

Mason stated the obvious. "You have to go back in there, or this phobia will have full control."

"That's easy for you to say—you don't have this phobia."

Mason took my hand. "I'll be with you in the room, so you will be fine."

CHAPTER 32

My stomach churned as I waited for the counsellor to call my name. Mason had been called into work and couldn't get out of it, so I was there on my own. Suddenly I heard my name: "Emily Brown."

I looked up and a woman was standing there. As I stood up, I gave a smile to acknowledge she had called me and followed her into a room. I sat down.

"Hi," she said. "My name is Claire and I work as a counsellor for the doctor's surgery. However, if I deem your case to be at a level that I consider to need more in-depth help, then I will refer you to someone else that may be able to help you further."

Nerves suddenly crept up on me. Even being in this room was an absolutely stupid idea. "I understand," I said quietly.

"Now, Emily, I have read your file and the comments that Dr Lane has made, but I'd like to hear from you why you are here today, so if you can talk me through what has been going on, hopefully then we can work on this together."

I started to fidget. "It all started a couple of weeks ago... No, wait, maybe a bit longer than that. Anyway, it started with dreams and, to be honest, I thought I was just having normal, run-of-the-mill nightmares, but they became more frequent and it was the same thing over and over. A figure, whose face I cannot see, they chase me down and then stab me. I don't know who the person is, but as they got worse, I accused my boyfriend of deliberately doing this to me. I saw the doctor after I freaked out in work because there were so many masks and Halloween decorations, and this was where I was told I had a phobia. Don't even asked me the name of this phobia because I can't pronounce it or them... I don't know. But that is why I'm here."

As I watched, the counsellor stayed silent for a few moments and then said, "It seems you have been through a lot. I just need to make you aware of something I did not say earlier, and that is that your time with me will be for a period of eight weeks as this is all I'm allowed to dedicate to each patient."

"OK." I nodded.

"What I am going to do over those weeks is to try and find out if we can pinpoint how this all occurred, and then I want to be able to bring in a mask into our session and see if we can overcome your fear."

I couldn't believe how matter-of-fact she was, but considering we only had a short amount of time together, I was willing to give anything a go. I just wanted my life back.

"We can try that," I replied with nerves.

"Good, now let me look in the diary and see when we can arrange our next appointment." She flipped a few pages through her book, and asked, "Is Friday OK with you?"

"Friday is fine. What time is available?"

When she looked back at her book, she told me that all day was available. I was about to say my preference when she added that she had an appointment from one o'clock in the afternoon onwards but she could do morning, so I arranged the appointment for ten-thirty.

I came out of the surgery feeling like nothing had been accomplished. Perhaps being the first appointment, that was normal. However, I'd expected a lot more. I didn't know—possibly an answer, maybe even a cure. I knew that was a bit of a stretch for a first appointment, but I just wanted this all to be over and to get back to normality. At that moment, I was getting the impression that there was no quick fix. I just hoped over the next eight weeks I'd get a resolution that I was pleased with.

Then I had a thought, *Shit, I forgot to tell her about the voices that I'm hearing… Well, maybe I'm hearing them.*

When I got home, I'd just fallen into the chair when I heard, "Trying to get help… pointless."

I bit my lip as I tried to ignore it.

"You know ignoring me won't help, because I'm still here."

Suddenly, I couldn't hold it in anymore.

"Listen," I shouted, "whoever you are, or whatever you are, I will beat you and this problem, so why don't you just give up now?"

Then I heard a cackling laugh. "We will see who is right, but only one will triumph."

CHAPTER 33

I went back to work and saw my manager, who had allowed me to go home the other day. She was tall and slim with bobbed brown hair and a nice golden tan.

"Hi," I said. "I just wanted to say thank you for letting me go home."

She looked at me with a smile that showed off her white teeth. "You did look shaken, so sending you home was the best option at that point. How are you now?"

"I'm good, thanks," I smiled back. "They think I might have a phobia, so they're trying to arrange some help."

"I'm pleased for you."

"Sooner rather than later, I hope," I said, smiling again.

As I walked away from her desk I wondered if I should have told her the counselling had started, but there was nothing to tell at this point.

I reached my desk, ripped down any decorations near or on it, calmly sat down and pressed the computer's 'on' button. My team were looking at me and my team leader approached. He was about five foot ten with short brown hair and a medium build—slim, but with a slight stomach on him—or as some men would call it, 'the beer belly'.

"Are you alright?" he asked.

I looked straight at him, keeping my expression calm and sarcastically replied, "After what happened the other day, I just don't want cobwebs and plastic bats on my desk."

He looked at me weirdly. "Let's go and talk about this."

I didn't have a choice, so I followed him down the aisle, passing the breakout area, and into a training room. We both sat down.

"Do you want to tell me what's going on?" he asked.

I looked at him with shock. "I left work early the other day due to a panic attack because there were lots of people in costumes and masks."

"I didn't know. Are you alright?"

"I did see the doctor and they're trying to get me into counselling, but I'm doing alright. I just didn't want all the decorations on my desk."

I wasn't trying to play things down, but I wasn't fully sure what was going on. Until I knew, and had the complete picture, I didn't want to elaborate any further.

"Emily, I get that you're getting help, but there's no need to snap and act aggressively within the workplace."

I was stunned—it felt like I was being told off—but I stayed calm. "As I said, I just didn't like the decorations on my desk."

"I understand that, but there is a way of removing the decorations without being aggressive."

I wanted to bite, but I held back. "I'll remember that next time."

When we came out of the room, he went one way and I went back to the team and my desk. Everyone was on calls, so I just sat there, logged in and started taking calls.

My team leader hadn't shown any empathy, just told me off. It was hard for that not to hurt. All because I'd cleared my desk of crap decorations.

A little while later, my friend Nancy sat by me.

"Are you OK?" she asked.

I finished the call and turned to her. "I've had better days. He just said to me not to act aggressively, all because I took the decorations down."

Nancy looked stunned. "He what?! You just looked like you were in a rush to get the decorations down—there was nothing aggressive about it."

"Well, he seems to think so. I'm just staying out of his way today. I really need to look for a new job, but for the time being, I'm stuck here. Everyone is great, it's just the management... Well, some of them. I just wish they showed more compassion."

Leo, my team leader, walked past and said, "Shouldn't you be at your desk taking calls?"

Nancy looked at him and replied flatly, "I was just checking that Emily was OK."

"Then I suggest you do it on your own time— for example, break."

She looked at me and said quietly so he couldn't hear, "Fucking team leader... Who does he think he is?"

I gave half a smile. "Thanks for coming over, but I think we'd better get back to taking calls before we're both in more trouble."

When I started taking calls again, I checked the clock. That was the worst thing I could have done—most of my shift was left and, after the way I'd been spoken to, all I wanted to do was get home and get out of this place.

CHAPTER 34

I met Mum for a meal after work. I started browsing the menu to decide what I wanted and that's when the interrogation started.

"So, how is Mark?"

I looked up. "He's doing well."

She gave me that look. "Does he have a job?" she prompted. "I do try ringing, but he won't pick up the phone to me."

"Mum, he's a grown man...most of the time. But he's just trying to find his way and, in some way, I have to admire him because at least he's not stuck in a dead-end job he hates."

The waiter came over, interrupting the flow of conversation.

"I'll have a latte," my mum said, "but I'm still thinking about what I'm going to eat. Emily, what are you going to drink?"

I made eye contact with the waiter. "I'll have a latte as well, please, but I need more time to look at the menu."

After the waiter left, Mum looked at me and picked up where we'd left off. "Find his way... really, Emily...you always have had a soft spot when it comes to that brother of yours. He needs a job and he needs to settle down."

I shook my head in disbelief. "He can't just settle down to please you. Plus, Mark is looking for a job."

Mum was getting frustrated with my responses.

"Fine, Emily. Have it your way. How are things with you?"

The waiter returned with our drinks and then I replied, "Mason and I had a fight and he stormed out because of what I did, but now we're talking again and taking things slower."

"I wasn't aware you'd had a fight. What was the fight about?"

"I thought that Dad might have told you..."

"Well, your dad and I are talking again, but he didn't mention anything, so tell me what's going on."

I quickly browsed the menu before answering. "I thought I saw a knife in his bag and because of the nightmares I've been having I accused him of trying to kill me. Dad was there, and I did try and ring Mason and apologise but he wouldn't answer his phone, and Dad told me to give him some time because I had hurt him."

Mum interlocked her fingers together and sat up straight. "Emily, you have a wonderful boyfriend and you go and accuse him of something so horrible... How could you?" I was about to speak when she added, "Just as well your dad was there as well."

I rested my head in my hand as I shook it back and forth. "You're right—I have a great boyfriend, and yes, I was stupid—but with these nightmares getting worse I lost it and straight away I regretted it, but I am one lucky person because Mason is talking to me again and still wants to be with me."

As the evening progressed, Mum not only interrogated me but lectured me on how to keep a boyfriend. She did have some good points—I wouldn't deny that—but she went on and on, and then came the ultimate question:

"So, when are you and Mason getting married?"

I almost choked on my food. "Mason hasn't asked me to marry him, so the answer to your question would be I don't know, but we're thinking of moving in together."

It was like I'd given my mum a Christmas present. She started beaming.

"Finally, you and Mason living together. Personally, I'd prefer you both being married, but I'll take living together."

"Mum!"

"What? I'm just being honest. Besides, I just want you to be happy, and you seem really good together. Now, if your brother becomes as happy as you with someone, then I will finally be really happy."

My mum meant well, but sometimes she was too much.

"I know what you're saying, but you really need to back off a bit. The living together is still in discussion—we haven't even started looking at houses yet, or if I'm gonna move in with him or if he's moving in with me."

"If you want my advice…"

"Which I don't need."

"…I would say you need to get a new place together. That way, it would stop all the arguments. Because if he moved in with you then you'd be saying, 'Don't move this, don't move that,' and it would make him feel as if it wasn't his home, and vice versa, but it's just my opinion. You will do what you want to do."

CHAPTER 35

I walked in the door and Mason was in the living room.

"Hey," I said.

He smiled at me. "How was dinner with your mum?"

"It was nice," I replied, cuddling into him. "Just, she interrogated me about Mark and about us."

"Nothing unusual then."

I kissed him and he kissed me back, softly but passionately. I pulled away.

"Can we stay at yours tonight?" I asked quietly. "Because with Mark and his new girlfriend, it's a bit crowded for alone time."

He pulled me back into a kiss and his strong arms wrapped around me. "Alone time sounds like fun."

"I didn't mean it like that."

He lifted his eyebrow. "Maybe not, but I might want to…"

Then he started kissing me again, and as the kiss grew more intense and passionate, I glimpsed something out of the corner of my eye. I pushed Mason away to look.

"Is something wrong?" Mason asked.

I just kept staring towards where I'd seen something.

"Em."

Suddenly, I snapped out of the trance I was in. "Sorry. I thought I'd seen something."

He looked disappointed. "It would be a good

time to pack a few things. Then we can get going."

I agreed and went upstairs to gather my things.

As I put the last of my things into a bag, I heard a creak. I quickly turned and noticed my wardrobe door was wide open. I closed the door and grabbed my bag. Another noise came from the window. I rushed over to investigate. I'd left it open—something must have pressed up against it to make the noise. I closed the window and went downstairs to meet Mason at the front door.

"Are you ready?" he asked.

"Just a sec…" I sent a text to Mark to let him know he had the place to himself for the night. "Just letting Mark know I won't be here."

Mason had already headed to the car. I got in and remembered I'd left my cigarettes on the kitchen table.

"Hang on—I have to get my fags."

"Then hurry up." Mason sounded impatient.

I slammed the door as I got out and went back inside. The kitchen was dark. As I approached the table, a slight breeze brushed past my neck, as if something was behind me. Panic set in and I froze on the spot. I slowly picked up my cigarettes and, as I turned to walk out, I saw an outline in the window. I turned quickly, but no one was behind me. When I looked back at the window, the outline of something was still there.

My breathing grew slow and shallow as I approached the back door. I opened the door and the outline grew closer, becoming more solid, more real, until it was the figure from my dream. I backed away, but as always, the figure kept my pace. Then his face came into focus for the first time. It was the man from the film, *Halloween*.

I wanted to scream but it was like someone had taken my voice. I ran into the hall and, when

I looked back, the man was gone. My heart was trying to escape my chest.

I was sat on the stairs, trying to catch my breath, when Mason walked back into the house.

"Em, what the hell is taking…" He stopped when he saw the state I was in. "Fuck's sake, Em. What's wrong? You look like you've been running a marathon."

I took my head out of my hands, and with a quiver in my voice, replied, "The figure was in the kitchen. I opened the back… and he walked inside… It looks like *Halloween*…" I trailed off unable to say anything more.

Mason sat next to me, resting his hand on my knee. "Em, you aren't making sense. Take a deep breath and start again."

I didn't look at him but did as he suggested and tried to explain again. "I came to get my fags—"

"By the way, you should quit."

I turned to glare at him. "Do you want me to explain? And I'll quit when I'm ready and not before."

"Sorry. Go on."

"I'd got them, but felt something behind me, and when I looked out the window in the kitchen, I saw the figure. I wanted to see if what I was seeing was really there, and when I opened the back door, the figure came inside, and that's when I saw the face for the first time, and as I said, it was *Halloween*."

He squeezed my hand. "Are you sure nothing is in the house?" he asked calmly.

I pulled my hand away. "I know what I saw," I snapped.

"I get that, but there's nothing here and—hear me out—but could it be your imagination playing tricks on you?"

"I've changed my mind," I said firmly, walking away. "I'm staying here and not at your place."

"Fine, but I'm not going home, Em, so don't try to push me away."

"Do whatever," I shouted back.

CHAPTER 36

I was sat on my bed, seething, when Mason walked in.

"You need to control this," he said, "and stop pushing me away."

"Control this… And how do I do that? Do you have any idea of what this is like?"

He stayed by the bedroom door but snapped back, "No, but I do know you are letting this control you, and it's affecting us."

I stood up and stepped closer. "I am not—"

"Oh, really? Because when we were kissing downstairs, you pushed me away because you thought you saw something."

"I did see something…"

"Or was that an excuse to not kiss me?"

"What!? This isn't about you."

"I know, as it's all about you and this phobia."

I saw red. "Look, you said you believed me. You even said you looked up the phobia and it's a real thing."

"I did, but that doesn't change the fact that you're letting it control you. Every five minutes, it's something, and we haven't had sex in ages—"

I interrupted him before he could say anything more. "So this argument is really about you not getting any."

"I never said that…"

"Yes, you did."

"OK, I did, but come on, you have to admit, I can't kiss you without you thinking or seeing things… This phobia, it's driving me crazy."

"You think that it's a picnic for me!? Well, it's not. It's great I have a name for it, but you think I want to be this messed-up person? I don't; I wish I could rewind the clock to before all this crap started, but I can't, and us at each other's throats isn't helping."

"If we could go for a minute without all this crap then it would be a start."

"Just leave me alone for a bit," I said as I turned away from him.

"Fine—have it your way."

The bedroom door slammed. I went up to the door but didn't open it. Something had to change.

* * *

It was my first proper session in counselling and I was nervous. Claire smiled reassuringly.

"I looked into this condition a bit more," she said, "and I have come up with a plan for the next eight weeks. Today, we will discuss in depth how you feel when this phobia presents itself, and hopefully we will discover what can trigger it. Then in our next appointment, I want you to get a mask from somewhere so we can work on you being in the same room as the mask, and then we will go on from there. Is this OK with you?"

I'd been backed up against a wall with no choice, but I replied, "That sounds great. Hopefully I'll be alright after this." This was my hope anyway.

I started from the beginning as I knew it. "I walked into the living room when I was four and saw a man slice another man, and he was wearing a mask—this was on telly. I remember screaming and trying to find my parents. Things were calm after that, and then my parents took me to the fairground one summer and Dad bought a helmet with an opening for the mouth. He put it on, poked his tongue through and I screamed. I do remember my parents were shocked at my reaction, but Dad removed the helmet straight away and I never saw it after that."

"You say it was a helmet and not a mask. How are you with helmets now?"

I was puzzled by the question, but answered, "I've been to museums where they display armour, and watched programmes with helmets in, and I have no reaction."

"And what about when you walked in on that horror film? What was your parents' reaction?"

"I don't remember. They probably were concerned, but beyond that I have no memory. Although it's only recently that I have started to remember the memories about the masks."

She was making notes. I dreaded what she could be writing. She might think I was making everything up, might not believe me at all.

"Anything else that you can remember?" she said.

"I can remember my mum made a witch's outfit when I was about ten years old, which I liked, but then she gave me this plastic crooked nose that smelt horrible when I put it on. She put a bit of talc in it, I think, to make it smell better, but it made me feel sick, so I purposely broke the string so I couldn't wear it."

"Was this costume for Halloween?"

I nodded. "Yes. A few friends from the street were going trick-or-treating and they wanted me to go."

"Did you want to go?"

"Not really, but I went anyway."

She continued to write. "So this was on Halloween, but did anything else happen?"

I thought for a moment. "I remember a horror was on the TV...a bed in the middle of a field, and as someone goes near it—I suppose to pull back the covers—a man with pale skin...a vampire, I think, jumps up, and I scream and run into the hallway."

"You have very good memories of these incidents that have taken place—that's good. Unfortunately, we have come to the end of the session, so don't forget to get a mask, and I'll see you next Wednesday?"

"That's fine. See you then."

CHAPTER 37

I rang my friend to tell her what had happened at counselling and ask if she had a mask or if she knew anyone who did. Her son had one from Halloween and she agreed to let me borrow it. I told her to wrap it up so I wouldn't see it when I took it into the session. She told me that wasn't a problem and she would see me next week.

When I collected the mask from her, it was wrapped in a bin bag. I threw it into the back of the boot and headed to the surgery.

I took a deep breath, grabbed the bin bag and headed inside. When I was in the office, the counsellor asked, "Were you able to get a mask?"

I showed her the bin bag and said, "The item is in here."

She smiled. "Where did you get the mask?"

"I asked my friend if she had one and she did. She said it belongs to her son."

"Great. Before we start, just to let you know, the doctor had a response from the hospital in regards to getting you more tailored help for your phobia, and they've turned you down."

Her words shocked me and for a moment my words were lost. "Why? The doctor says I need the help because it's affecting my daily life."

"I agree with the doctor—you need more tailored help and, as you know, our sessions are only for a limited amount of time, whereas going through the hospital, you would get the help you needed for as long as you needed it and not on a timetable, so the doctor is going to write to them again. However, we do have a session, and I'd like to be able to help you if I can, so what I'm now going to do is open up the bin bag with the mask in it, and I want you to concentrate on your breathing while looking at the mask over on the bed. Do you think you are ready for this?"

"I'm really not sure. Now I've got a name for this problem, I don't know that I want to face it... but I also want my life back." I took a deep breath. "I'm ready, I think... No. I *am* ready."

Trying to keep my emotions under control, I watched as she ripped open the bin bag.

She looked at me. "Now, I want you to look at the mask, but I also want you to concentrate on your breathing, taking deep breaths as you look at it. Now you need to turn to the mask."

I slowly turned my head towards the bed and took my first look. It was a red devil mask. My stomach turned as I started to feel sick. Panic swept over as the fear built inside me and I started to sweat.

I heard Claire say, "What are you feeling right now?"

I kept staring. "I don't want to be in the same room as this mask," I said quietly. "I feel sick and I want to run."

"These are all normal responses for a phobia. But if you breathe, you may feel OK in a few moments."

The feeling was building; my anxiety levels were through the roof. I tried to concentrate on my breathing, but nothing was working. The fear was overwhelming. I tried to tear my eyes away from it, but I couldn't—it was like it was daring me to have a staring competition with it.

In the end, I had to say, "Please put it away—I

can't do this anymore… Please."

"I do understand, and I will cover it." As she covered the mask, she added, "You should be proud of yourself, as you have done really well today. This is definitely a step in the right direction."

Once the mask was covered, I asked, "Would it be OK if the surgery kept this safe until my friend can come and collect it?"

"That should be fine. Just make sure your friend can pick it up in a few days, if that's OK."

I was relieved when she agreed. "I'll ring her when I leave and then she can collect it."

We made arrangements to have another session the following week, but I really was starting to feel that this was a pointless exercise. I didn't feel any better, but then again, this had been my first real test. To be fair, this was still early days.

"Before you go, I just wanted to let you know that after the eight weeks with me, I have arranged for you to go to a support group. It's for different things, from phobias to alcohol, and they will help you through relaxation techniques so you can keep your fears and anxieties under control. A better way to manage them."

"That's fine. I mean, I'll take anything at this point. I'll see you next week."

CHAPTER 38

I was cooking dinner when Mason walked in shouting, "Hello."

"Hello," I shouted back.

He wandered into the kitchen, came up to me and kissed me. We had sorted things out, but things still didn't feel right. Maybe that was just me.

He grabbed a bottle of wine out of the fridge, poured us both a glass and sat down. "So, are we going to talk about moving in together properly?"

I glanced at him briefly. "You still want us to move in together?"

"Of course." He had a puzzled look on his face. "What made you think otherwise?"

After I'd finished checking on the food, I turned back around. "I just thought with all the up-and-down incidents we've had that maybe you would change your mind."

"Em, I haven't changed my mind, and that's why I want to discuss this with you properly over dinner. I mean, I can give up my place and move in here, but I think we agreed when we talked about it initially that we would get a property together."

I sat down next to him. "Mum said something the other day when we were out for food, and I think she's right: getting a place of our own rather than you moving here or vice versa would be the better option."

He leaned over and kissed me with a smile. "I think your mum is very smart," he said sweetly.

I went back to the oven and checked on the food, taking my glass of wine with me.

"How did the session go today?" Mason asked.

"I had to look at a mask—the one that Stacy lent me. Anyway, I felt sick when looking at it."

"How do you feel now that you've broken the ice with the mask, so to speak?"

I looked at him and sighed. "I feel worse. I just get the feeling that things aren't going to change."

He took a sip of his wine. "Now who's being negative? Think positive, as things will change, believe me."

"I hope you are right," I said, sitting back down, "but I still have my doubts. Also, they've arranged for me to go to some support group to help with relaxation techniques, I think…something like that." I checked on the food once more. "Can you set the table? Because food is ready."

I served up the food and we sat and talked about work for a little bit.

Then Mason asked again, "So how are we going to tackle this moving in together?"

"I think the best thing to do is go to estate agents and see what is out there first, and then maybe see a bank manager about getting a mortgage together. Then, if all goes well, we both can put our properties on the market."

"You do remember I rent…right?"

I smiled at him. "Sorry, I forgot that, but you know what I meant."

"Yes, I knew what you meant." He touched my hand and smiled. "I'm free tomorrow if you want to go and look at the estate agents and see what they have."

"I'm working tomorrow, but only in the morning, so we can go after two o'clock."

Mason finished off what he was eating and

then replied, "I'll pick you up, and then we can go straight from there."

"I'm looking forward to it. So, does this mean you can get rid of all your stuff that you have in the flat?"

Suddenly, he just stared at me. "Hang on— you expect me to get rid of all my stuff and live with your things? No offence, Em, but I like my stuff, and besides, we could always get rid of your things and keep mine."

I almost choked on my food. "I'm not getting rid of anything." Mason gave a little smile, and I continued, "Alright, maybe I can get rid of a few things, but we'll have to sort something out, otherwise this living together will not happen."

Mason just put his glass down and said to me, "Look, I think the best way to tackle this is to look at what can go in the bin that's either broken or about to fall apart, then go from there."

He had a point, but this was something we were going to work on because I really did want to move in with him. At some point, there would be things I'd have to compromise on, but at least we were on the same page about where we wanted to be, and that was living together. However, I knew one thing for sure: that sofa in his flat was definitely going to the skip. I just hoped he understood.

CHAPTER 39

After dinner, Mason and I cuddled up on the sofa. I was almost asleep when I felt his hand stroke my hair. After a few minutes, I lifted my head.

"Do you want to continue this upstairs?" I asked softly.

He smiled and cupped my face, bringing us closer together. When he was just inches from my lips, he said in a whisper, "I want you, Em."

For a moment, I closed my eyes and then looked into his. They screamed excitement. "Mason, would you stay here permanently while we look for a place of our own?"

"Yes."

Then he kissed me slowly, and once our lips parted, he grabbed my hand and led the way. When we got to the bedroom, my energy was suddenly renewed. We couldn't keep our hands off each other as the clothes dropped to the floor. We fell onto the bed and his lips started to explore my body. My body reacted to him, and I wanted to slow down and enjoy this, but at the same time, I wanted us to consume each other. It had been a while since we'd had this intense need for each other. Then, without warning, Mason was inside me. I had to admit, it felt really good. I really needed this, and him, so badly.

* * *

Mason

I checked the time—Emily would be at work for a few more hours.

"Are you talking to me?" Mark asked, walking in.

I just looked at him. "Lisa here?"

"No, why?"

That was when I spoke freely. "You nearly blew things for me…"

"Look, I'm sorry. Have you bought a ring yet?"

"I've been looking, but something keeps stopping me."

"Fucking get a grip. You either love my sister or you don't—it's that simple."

"Then tell me why you aren't married!"

"That's different, and we aren't talking about me, are we? Look, all I'm saying is that if you love her—and by the noise coming out of the room last night, I'd say you do—and before you say anything, it's not an image I wanted as it's my sister, but anyone can see you love each other."

Knowing he'd heard us made me want to cringe. "Sorry you heard. But you're right—I am crazy about her. It's just this phobia stuff and all the crap that goes with it."

"About that phobia, my parents had an idea, not that it was a phobia but that Halloween wasn't a favourite time of year for her. When Emily stopped mentioning the nightmares, they put it to the back of their minds, thinking no more about it until recently. Also, I've spoken to them both and I'm keeping them updated about the help she is getting. Plus, Dad did tell me about Emily's freak-out and what she accused you of."

"You knew…"

"Another confession… I was told by Dad to

stay here to make sure Emily was fine. I tried to stay with Dad, but because this happened, he said to come here instead."

"So, tell me, Mark, do you actually have a place?"

"No, and don't be angry…"

"I'm just angry that they haven't told Emily the truth about knowing something about her nightmares."

"Look, Mum said never to bring it up, and Dad—after what happened with you—wanted to make sure she was OK."

In truth, Mark was right about keeping an eye on Emily, but I wasn't going to tell her that or I'd be in the doghouse.

"So, how are things going with Lisa?" I asked.

"She's OK. I may keep her around for a few weeks."

I shook my head. "Mark, you're something else, do you know that?"

He smiled. "What can I say? But it's never a dull moment with me. I might decide to settle down, but we will see. Now, haven't you got to get my sister?"

I looked at the clock. "Shit, I'm late." I grabbed my jacket as I ran out the door.

When I pulled up outside Emily's work, she didn't look impressed. It had been raining and she didn't have a coat.

"Why are you late?"

"Sorry, Em, I got talking with Mark and lost track of time."

She scowled at me, but her look softened. "You are lucky I love you. Do you still want to go to the estate agents?"

"Just because it's raining, you think I'd go home…uh, no. Let's go to the high street and see what they have."

CHAPTER 40

Emily

When we got home, I was exhausted—so many estate agents. Mason and I had seen a few houses we liked, but one thing that struck me was that some of the estate agents said to us that, because we were a young couple, we should look for a minimum of three bedrooms, not only from a selling point of view, but in case we wanted children. I'd had enough stress lately and now someone had mentioned children. People needed to back off—we weren't ready for family life just yet.

As I looked around my house, thinking about putting it up for sale, I realised how much I loved it. It was the first home I'd bought and it held so many memories—good and bad—and soon it would belong to someone else.

I had to check my emails, so I opened my browser on my laptop. Suddenly, I felt sick. There was a picture of someone dressed up as Scream, from the film. Terror froze my body. I tried to move the mouse to get it off the screen, I couldn't take my eyes away—I was afraid if I did something would happen. I started to panic, tears running down my cheeks and my body shaking. Finally, I clicked off the article, but it was too late. I was terrified.

I ran from the room and found Mason watching TV. He saw me.

"What happened?" he asked.

At first, I didn't say anything, just rushed over and embraced him.

"I saw a mask on the computer screen."

He just held me until I calmed down.

"When is your next appointment?" he said as he looked at me.

"Next week."

"Is it working?"

"I don't know."

"It just seems that it's not working," he said, still holding me.

"It's early days, so I'm hoping it will." I wiped my face and changed the subject. "So what houses did you prefer? Did you want to look at any?"

"I liked all I saw, but we need to know what we can borrow first, and don't forget I rent."

"Why did you rent?"

"I'd never lived on my own and the thought of a mortgage seemed like too much work."

"You have a good job."

"I didn't when I first rented the flat, so renting was the best option."

I was enjoying feeling normal when a fear came over me like a sixth sense. I heard that voice again, taunting me. But then I heard the door and Lisa walked in. Mark had given her a key—why would he do that?

"Where's Mark?" I asked.

"He gave me the key—hope that is OK?" I wasn't impressed. Then she added, "I bought this for Mark."

That was when I had a panic attack. She held out a horror film and the sight of the cover filled me with dread. All these feelings that I'd experienced built up in me.

"Get that out of my house."

She looked shocked. "It's a film—get a grip."

Why didn't she understand? Maybe Mark hadn't explained, but I didn't care. All I knew was that film had to be out of here.

"I said get it out of my house."

Ignoring me, she went to go upstairs, but my fear and panic had escalated past caring.

"I'll put it another way: get out of my house and take that film with you."

"This is Mark's place, so no."

I tried to stay calm—well, stay sane—and was about to answer, when Mason said, "This is Em's house, not Mark's, so as my girlfriend said, get out of her house. And in case you were wondering, you aren't allowed back here either."

The look on her face was priceless. It was the first time I'd heard Mason defend me like that.

After Lisa left, I turned to Mason. "Thank you," I said calmly.

He smiled at me. "You looked pale, and that wasn't good, and you were trembling, so I had to step in. How are you now?"

"I'm getting back to normal, I think."

CHAPTER 41

As the weeks went by, the counselling sessions didn't seem to be helping. They weren't giving me the help I needed. When I'd started going to the sessions, I'd thought it could help and I could get better, but now all I could think was that they were a waste of time.

The last session came, and my counsellor Claire said, "When you first walked in the door, I thought this was something I could help you with. However, it is very clear that this phobia isn't common, and it is something I've never come across personally, so due to my lack of experience in this area, I unfortunately don't think I have helped. But I will be writing to the hospital and explaining the situation. Hopefully they will take you on, so they can help you."

"Is this phobia treatable then?"

"I don't see why not, but—as I said—because I've never come across this particular phobia in the past and it is rare, I really do think that the hospital would be better suited to helping you."

"When you write to them, how long do you think it will be before we get an answer back from them?"

"I think we should hear from them in somewhere from six to eight weeks, as they will need time to read the report that I will be sending them, and because they've already heard from your doctor as well, this should enable them to have the bigger picture."

Panic started to set in. "So in the meantime I have to live with this and be frightened each time?"

"Due to the nature of the phobia, it appears to be a seasonal issue, and therefore you should only suffer at that time of year."

"I'm not sure it is seasonal, because I was suffering before Halloween arrived, and shortly after."

She looked at me sympathetically. "I think it is seasonal. Having said that, if masks were to show up at any point during the year, then you may experience discomfort. I know it is not a pleasant experience for you, but unfortunately, due to the hospital turning you down the first time, this is now a waiting game."

"Yes, I understand it's a waiting game. However, I am the one that's suffering while I'm waiting for the hospital to accept that I need help. What if they refuse to help me again?"

She thought for a moment. "If that happens then I suggest that you see your doctor about the phobia and get them to try the hospital again."

I came out of there deflated. The sessions hadn't worked and I felt no different, but I hoped the course she had put me forward for would help me control my emotions and help me relax if I saw anything in the future. Until then, I was stuck in limbo with this phobia that I could not pronounce.

When I got home, Mason was unpacking the last of his boxes.

"Well, now I'm unpacked," he said, "and I've paid the last on the flat, so now it can be rented to someone else."

"Did the bank get back to us?"

"Yes—we can borrow up to one hundred and sixty thousand pounds."

I was shocked. "Is that combined?"

"Yep… How did the session go?"

I headed out to the kitchen and Mason followed. "The first few sessions, I thought I had a chance, but for the last couple of weeks, I've seen no point in going. The hospital won't take me on, so the counsellor is writing to them again in the hopes that they will take this more seriously. In the meantime, I have to live with it the best I can, so I'm back at square one."

"You have me," Mason said, taking over making my drink, "and your family, and we want to help, so you're not at square one. We know what it is, and even though we may not fully understand, we will support you."

I had to admit, his support was nice to have. I didn't understand the full extent of my phobia, so this was a learning curve for both of us, but things had calmed down. I hadn't heard the voice in weeks, the nightmares were gone and I hadn't seen anything in a while. Mason and I were moving on. I just hoped all the bad things that had happened to me would stay in the past.

CHAPTER 42

The next few months went smoothly with no incidents and it felt great. Mason and I bought a house together, but unfortunately it came with a housemate, my brother, who couldn't find a place because no one would let him rent until he had a good employment history. He dumped that girl he was seeing, which was a relief. He finally got a job and was finally paying his way. He'd started seeing someone else—it had lasted three weeks so far and things were looking up. I met her once, and I'm happy to say she didn't stay over at all.

Mason also got a promotion, but it meant he had to move to a different store with a longer commute. Neither of us was happy about that, but that's how things go at times.

My appointment with the doctor came around and I explained to him what had been happening. "On the lead-up to Halloween, I thought I was seeing things, even as far as hearing voices. Then I had an incident in work last year. I saw a doctor and I was told I had a phobia, which explained a lot. I saw the surgery counsellor, and that didn't help, and I'm still waiting on support sessions the counsellor was on about, but I haven't heard anything. I also haven't heard from the hospital about seeing a psychiatrist. It's just, I want help before it comes around again."

I felt like I hadn't taken a breath. The doctor looked at the computer screen and read the comments from the other doctor. He turned back to me. "You were advised it was a phobia, and I can see a letter was sent to the hospital, but they turned your case down. The counsellor did send another letter, but again it was rejected. I will send another letter to them, stressing the point you need to be seen, and I will check on the support sessions the counsellor suggested for you. The voices you mentioned—are they talking to you all the time?"

"No, it's not like that. The best way I can explain it is…it's like having a bad dream, awake or asleep, and you are having a conversation, but in my case, it taunts me. I don't hear voices in that sense. I hope I've made sense?"

"OK, that's fine, but if that changes, please come back to the surgery."

"I will." I was just glad he understood what I was trying to say.

"In the meantime, if things get too much then let us know."

"Thank you, and I will."

As I left, my life felt on hold, but there was nothing I could do about it. I just had to get on with it, and that was what scared me, as I didn't have control over the phobia.

When I got to work the following day, I requested to speak to my team leader. We went into a private room and I asked if anything could be done to avoid the panic I'd had in work all those months back. He told me I could take time off from my holiday allocation.

It was a start, but I asked, "Could I have a warning about when the decorations go up?"

He looked puzzled. "How are we going to do that exactly?"

I thought for a moment. "Ring me or let me

know beforehand when they go up so I'm not here."

He didn't seem impressed, or to care much about what I'd been through. "I can see if that's possible, but you are here to work and this is a business."

"I understand that, but I don't want to go through anything like that again. I'm just trying to think of ways to help myself while I'm waiting to get help."

"Well, I can see what I can do, and then I will get back to you."

He really didn't care and I thought he was just trying to say the right words so he could leave and get back to doing nothing. However, I smiled.

"Thanks, and just let me know as soon as you can."

"I will. Now, is there anything else you need from me?"

I hated that line—it always sounded belittling and made me feel as if I was wasting their time.

I just smiled back, "Not today."

CHAPTER 43

A week later, my doctor called and advised me the support sessions that the counsellor had put me forward for had come through. It was a stress-control course designed to help find ways of coping and dealing with stressful situations. It was a six-week course and I had to attend every single one. If I did not attend, then my doctors would be informed.

A few weeks later, I arrived at the building where the stress course was taking place. The lady taking the session introduced herself and explained how the course would work. Apparently, she was a 'stress tutor' and each week we would tackle something new. We'd work through a workbook each week and she'd ask each of us to tell the group why we were there. Then, as we worked through the workbooks, we'd take notes of what could work best for our situation and work on it. Then, the following week, we would discuss if that particular technique had helped us or not and move to the next workbook.

Once the workbooks had been handed out, I felt overwhelmed by the size of them—there was a lot of information to take on board.

As she went through the workbook, I listened to why other people were there. It suddenly dawned on me that this course might not work for me. Everyone was there for a reason, but nobody's was the same as mine. All the advice in this booklet seemed to cater for people under stress.

During the break, I went up to the tutor. "I don't think this session is going to work for me."

She held her cup of coffee in her hands. "Name? I haven't met you before?"

"Sorry, it's Emily Brown."

"I read about your situation," she said, smiling, "and I have to say, it is different. I can understand why you may think this won't help, but I suggest staying on the course because you may find helpful tips on how to control your attacks."

After the break, we went into more detail about what triggered stress for each of us, but for me, I wasn't having any of my usual anxiety as we weren't approaching Halloween. Then we were asked to keep a diary until the next week. We were to determine how stressed we were from day to day, say why and score it from one to ten.

My diary for the first week:

Day One: My brother not cleaning up in the kitchen. Score 4.

Day Two: Mason leaving his clothes on the floor. Score 4.

Day Three: Hate the job when customers swear at me. Score 6.

Day Four: Same as yesterday and brother asked to borrow money. Score 6.

Day Five: Horrible day at work. Score 7.

Day Six: Another crappy day at work. Score 6.

I left day seven blank, as I was going to the meeting then.

"How are you feeling about the session this evening?" Mason asked.

"I honestly don't know. I know I've only had week one and this will be week two, but it feels like nothing is relevant to my situation. The people in the session with me are people that are dealing with depression, loss of relationships and other things. They all seem to have things in common, and then there's me, who has a completely different situation."

"The best thing you can do is just keep trying these meetings—something might become relevant and help. I mean, you have to give it a shot after what the doctor told you."

"I know, but it's frustrating because I just want the help. Work don't seem to take this seriously, so I don't know what is going to happen next time, when Halloween is getting closer."

"Well, you did say that the manager saw the fear on your face, and hopefully a few team leaders will talk to the manager, then they'll understand and help you."

"I hope you're right, but I just get the impression that they either don't care or they don't understand and, if I'm honest, it's probably both. I guess I'll have to wait and see, but I hope you're right and they want to help."

I was going to be late if I didn't get going, so I gave Mason a kiss on the cheek and said sweetly, "I'll see you in a few hours—and make sure Mark does his dishes."

CHAPTER 44

I turned up for week two and the tutor laid out the plan for that night. She talked to the group about 'getting rid of the things that make you worse', focussing on alcohol and tablets. If we used either of these to cope with stress, we should stop.

I sat there, thinking I was definitely on the wrong course. She talked about how to relax, breathing and controlling your body. She provided a relaxation disc and wanted us to keep a diary of our relaxation. 'What were our stress levels before the relaxation disc?' and 'What our levels were like after we played the disc?'

I was getting nowhere—my stress levels were fine at the moment so I really didn't know how I would tackle this.

When I got home, I went straight to the bedroom and listened to the disc. It was alright. I looked through the week two booklet again and I found out that I had to carry on with the daily diary. It wouldn't be much different from the first week, but I'd promised that I would put in the effort and see if things worked for me. So, I kept the diary for another week.

Day One: My brother arguing with me and Mason still leaving his clothes on the floor. Score 5.

Day Two: Hate the job when customers swear at me. Score 6.

Day Three: Mason leaving plates on the table. Score 6.

Day Four: Horrible day at work as usual. Score 7.

Day Five: Mason and Mark arguing over watching their programmes on the telly. Score 6.

Day Six: Another crappy day at work. Score 6.

Day seven I left blank. I knew I shouldn't, but by then it was getting tedious because, really, I wasn't getting anything from this. However, I had been listening to the relaxation disc and it did seem to help me relax, but that wasn't why I was on the course. Normal stress levels didn't bother me and I wasn't that stressed out. Well, not at this time of year.

I looked at each item listed in the stress control glossary I'd been given. A few things stood out for me. The first was *insomnia*, difficulty in getting to sleep. It only applied to me nearer Halloween season—I didn't have problems throughout the rest of the year. My favourite one was *expectations*—what hopes did I have for the future? My hope was that I could get the right help and get cured so I wouldn't have to go through anything like that again.

The counselling I'd had so far and these sessions weren't tailored to my specific needs. It was like the doctors didn't know what they needed to do in order to help me. However, the positive spin on this was that it is what it is, and it will always be like this, but at least it wouldn't get any worse.

There was a knock on the bedroom door and Mason walked in.

I smiled. "Why did you knock?"

"You were listening to that disc you were on about."

"Relaxation disc. But this is your room."

"Yes, but I was giving you the time you needed

to listen to it in peace and quiet. Anyway, I'm meeting Paul soon, so I need to get changed."

"Is everything alright with your brother?"

"Not really," Mason replied, changing his shirt. "Paul and Rachel had a huge row. He sounds really upset."

"Do you know what's going on?"

"No, but by the way he said it, things sound bad, so I'm going to meet him and hopefully I'll find out what's going on. I'd hoped he'd text me to say it had all blown over."

"Say hi from me and see you later."

He kissed me. "Hopefully it won't be a late one, as I have work in the morning."

"See you later." I pulled him in for another kiss. "Now go and sort your brother out, and then get back here."

CHAPTER 45

I looked at the clock. It was one o'clock and Mason still wasn't home.

Suddenly, I heard the key in the lock and Mason stumbling up the stairs. He staggered into the room and muttered, "Should really decorate in here."

I turned the light on and he quickly made his way over to me. "Fancy having sex?"

"Mason, you're drunk. And besides, you have work."

He tried to kiss me, but I pushed him off. When his head hit the pillow, he fell asleep.

In the morning, he came downstairs, dressed for work but looking rough.

Holding a cup of strong coffee out to him, I said, "Morning… late night?"

He lowered his head slightly. "Not so loud. And please say that coffee is for me?"

Smirking, I handed the mug over.

"Em, don't look at me like that. I already know what you're going to say."

I raised an eyebrow. "Really? Because I was going to say that I agreed with you about decorating our bedroom."

"When did I mention that?"

I smiled. "When you stumbled through the bedroom door."

He finished his coffee. "Have to go," he said. "But we can talk about this later."

* * *

The next four weeks of the stress course went by quickly. The third week was about controlling your thoughts. We had to keep a court case diary, listing the stressful thought, evidence for and against it, and the conclusion.

The fourth week was about controlling your actions and trying to deal with stressful emotions on the spot. The fifth week was about how to control your breathing with a supplement on panic attacks.

When the final week came, it was about putting together everything we had learnt and how to use it to treat the stress we were experiencing. I even received a certificate for attending the stress-control course, which I was proud of, but how was that going to help me through my problem?

* * *

The months flew by. When I looked at the calendar, I couldn't believe it was September already.

In the team meeting at work, the team leader, Leo, said, "And the last thing to discuss is Halloween. I know, it has only just turned September, but I want ideas so we can concentrate on a theme."

I couldn't believe this. He knew how I felt, what I was like last year. I needed to say something, and quickly.

After the meeting, I approached Leo. "Can I have a word?"

He looked at me and replied, "I'm about to head into a meeting, so I'll have to speak to you later."

I was being blown off but, as usual, I replied with a smile. "Speak later."

Later came and went and Leo didn't come back to his desk. I was walking down the stairs, about to leave after another long day, when I saw him walk past.

"Leo!" I called after him and got his attention. "I wanted to talk to you earlier."

"Yes... Sorry about that, but the meeting took longer than expected. When you come in tomorrow, then we can talk."

"What time are you in?" I said, trying not to show my disappointment at being palmed off.

"I'm in at eight o'clock. I'm on the early shift."

"I'm in at eight-thirty, so can we talk then?"

"Remind me in the morning, but that should be fine."

"OK. Speak then."

As I left the building, I felt my anger grow. I got that team leaders could be busy, but it felt like they tried to run from me whenever I needed to speak to them. I just wanted to make sure things weren't going to repeat themselves, as I didn't want to go through that again, and I didn't want to miss work again either. All I could hope was that my team leader understood and something could be arranged.

CHAPTER 46

When I got to my desk, Leo was nowhere to be found, so I just logged in and did my job. An hour later, he arrived and signalled to me to go into a code so we could talk. I went over to his desk.

"Have a seat," he said.

I sat down and waited for him to speak.

"So you wanted to speak to me yesterday. How can I help?"

"In the team meeting, you mentioned about Halloween. I don't want a repeat of last year, so is there anything we can do to avoid that?"

"How do you mean?"

"Can I take time off work during this period and can the decorations be taken down before I return to work?"

"Taking time off work depends if there's any availability, and I'm not sure how we'd go about taking the decorations down before you returned."

"What if there's no availability?"

"Then you would be expected to be in work and fulfil your contract."

I tried to stay calm. "Is there any way we can check if there is availability?"

Leo didn't answer me straight away but looked on the computer. "There's limited availability. Do you have any holidays available?"

"I have about ten days available that I can take."

"You can book from twenty-ninth of October to first November off."

I was pleased to hear there was some availability. "Then I'll book those days off so everyone can have their fun."

"That's good. Now that's sorted, is there anything else?"

"No, that was it—thank you."

I returned to my desk, booked the dates that were available and hoped it would sort out the issue.

* * *

When I got home, Mason had just finished preparing our bedroom to be decorated. I hated this part—our things were everywhere and all I wanted to do was to lie on the bed and relax. Mason reassured me it wouldn't take long to do our room and not to worry.

I decided to go to the shops as window shopping was always fun. I went into a shop and looked around and, when I came out, I noticed the window was being decorated with Halloween decorations. It was September, not October. My stomach churned. I crossed the road to get further away and kept my head down as I quickly passed by, but then I started to cry. My heart started to quicken. I'd only caught a glimpse and my symptoms were already escalating. I felt powerless to do anything.

As I walked in the door, Mason saw my face and asked, "Em, what's wrong?"

"There was..." I replied, tone panicked, "window... mask..."

Mason looked at me strangely.

Before he could speak, I blurted out somewhat coherently, "Shop window had Halloween decorations and masks."

"Well, it is September…"

"Glad to see you understand!" I snapped back.

Mason backtracked. "Em, I didn't mean it like that. It's just working in a store means that it's the time we put out seasonal items so people can be prepared. In this case, Halloween."

"It's too early…"

Mason held me and softly answered, "Not for the retail business. And before you say anything, I know that doesn't help you."

I pushed him away. "I'm fine now, and hopefully this will be the only shop with a window dressing."

But it was only the start. Suddenly, my head was spinning, and I heard, "I'm back."

I tried not to show Mason that the voice was back by trying the breathing techniques from the stress course and focussing on anything else, but all I heard was, "You'll hear from me a lot more the closer Halloween gets."

Trying to ignore the voice, I continued with my breathing, but the voice continued.

CHAPTER 47

Mason and I needed to do a big food shop, so we went to our local supermarket. We were getting what we needed when we turned the corner and there it was—an aisle filled with Halloween decorations and horror masks. Suddenly, I felt like I was going to have a heart attack. I felt sick and sweat was pouring down me, but I felt cold. I stopped dead in my tracks, frozen to the spot, but if I wanted to be safe, I had to run. I started to cry.

Outside, I tried to light a cigarette, but my hands shook too much.

Mason appeared. "Are you OK?" he asked.

I shook my head, tears running down my face. "Will you finish the shopping?"

"Em, we can leave the shopping if you want?"

I shook my head. "No—we need food, so please just finish shopping."

He went back inside. I had finally lit a cigarette when something caught my eye—a mask, running towards me. All I could do was freeze, but before the mask got to me, a woman yelled, "Get back here! What have I told you about running off?"

She grabbed a hand and suddenly I realised it was a child running towards me, wearing a mask. After what had happened in the store, and now this masked child was running towards me, I was in a downward spiral. Tears ran down my face, I was sweating and my heart felt like it was coming out of my chest. All I wanted to do was curl up in a ball and make everything go away, but I was stuck there until Mason came out.

I needed to get to the car so I could get inside and be that much closer to locking the world out of my life. When I was opening the door, I saw the figure from my dreams reflected in the window. I quickly turned around. Like before, nothing was there. However, before I got into the car, I checked the back seats to make sure no one was there waiting for me. Once that was done, I climbed into the seat and locked all the doors. Then I buried my head in my lap and started to cry uncontrollably. Trying to control my breathing, all I could think was, *You are a grown woman and this is stupid. There is no logic to this, now get a grip*. My body wasn't listening. I was falling apart at the seams. There was no controlling this fear, this phobia, and that terrified me. I felt I had no control over my life and nobody seemed to care.

Suddenly, there was a tap at the window. I jumped, but when I looked it was Mason. I opened the door.

"Can you open the boot so I can put the shopping in, please?" he asked.

I opened the boot, staying in the car while Mason sorted the shopping.

When he got into the car, he asked, "How are you feeling?"

"How do you think I'm feeling? I just want to go home. Once you left me to go back in store, a mask came towards me, and it was only when I heard yelling that I realised it was a child in a mask. I was so frightened I thought my heart was going out of my chest and I can't stop shaking, even now."

"I'll get you home, where you feel safe," he said, holding my hand briefly.

When we got home, I tried to help unpack the bags, but my hands were still trembling. This experience had really shaken me. Mason told me to stop sorting the bags out and to sit down; I did as I was told and he made me a drink.

He handed me a cup of tea. "Drink this," he said firmly. "And before you say anything, yes, it does have a lot of sugar in, as sugar is good for shock, so hopefully this will help you."

I took a sip of the tea. "What about the shopping?"

"I'll sort the shopping out; you just need to calm down."

The doorbell rang. I went to answer it and the figure from my dreams was standing there. When I looked down, a shiny silver knife was in his hand.

CHAPTER 48

Panic swept over me. I screamed at the top of my voice and ran. I made my way through the hall and into the kitchen and, as I reached for the knife in the holder, he grabbed me by the throat and just squeezed. I dropped the knife as I tried to prise his hand from my neck, but his grip just got tighter.

He dropped me to the floor. When I looked up, he was hovering over me. I tried to hurry away, but he kept coming. I turned onto my stomach to pull myself up and back onto my feet, but a huge force pushed me back down.

I was face down, looking at the floor. Suddenly, I felt a sharp pain. A few seconds later, the sharp pain came back. Abruptly, there was no weight on me, so I started to crawl away, still screaming.

When I glanced back, I saw a pool of blood. I stopped crawling and was forced to turn around. I faced the figure, who now held a bloody knife, and I watched in horror as he plunged it into my chest.

As I tried to breathe, I coughed up blood. That didn't seem to matter to the figure as he kept plunging the knife into me over and over again. Then I saw the figure wore a mask. Panic took over and this overwhelming sense of terror swept across me.

The next thing I knew, I was bolt upright in bed, soaked in sweat. Everything was so real. Trembling, I started to cry. I looked over and Mason was still asleep next to me, so I switched the light on, made my way to the bathroom and closed the door. I slid down to the floor, and there I cried uncontrollably.

As I desperately tried to calm down, it was hard for me to control my breathing. After about five minutes, it started to work, but a noise out of the bathroom window not only made me jump but swept the terror over me again. The panic attack and the anxiety just became all the more heightened.

I still wasn't right after about half an hour, but I went back to the bedroom and climbed into bed. Mason was still fast asleep and unaware of what just happened. I didn't want to close my eyes, but I had to because I had work the following day, so I turned the light off and quickly snuggled up to Mason in the hopes that would help me drift off to sleep.

As I hugged Mason even tighter, there were noises at the window and a voice said, "It's great to be back. The more afraid you are, the stronger I get. I just dropped in to say thank you."

I couldn't believe the voice was thanking me, and it fed off my anxiety, this was all I needed. In the morning, I would ring the doctor's surgery to get another appointment, because this was getting worse, not better.

* * *

After a terrible night's sleep, I poured myself a very strong coffee and lit a cigarette.

Mark entered the room. "Emily, you look like shit."

He helped himself to one of my cigarettes as I replied, "I had really bad nightmares. So yes, I've had a really bad night, and I'm a little tetchy, so lay off me."

"Are you alright?"

"What do you think?"

"I was just asking a question—there's no need to snap at me."

I took a sip of my coffee. "Sorry, Mark, I didn't mean to snap at you. Mason doesn't even know what happened last night because he slept all the way through it, and he's still asleep."

"I can tell him, if you want."

"Thanks—that will be a great help, as I've got to get off to work."

Before I walked out the door, I picked up the phone and made another appointment with the doctor to see him after work.

* * *

When the doctor called me in and I explained why I was there, he said, "We have finally heard back from the hospital and they have agreed to see you. However, you could possibly be waiting up to a year for the appointment."

Shock stabbed through my initial relief. When I spoke, my voice brimmed with panic. "A year? But I don't think I can wait that long. How I can cope until then?"

"If it gets too difficult, I can always sign you off work, and if the nightmares are too much, I can prescribe sleeping tablets, but only for a week."

I was happy that the doctor was on board with my phobia and believed how bad things were, but I wasn't sure about sleeping tablets. I did agree that, if it got any worse, I would come back and speak to him. Even though I'd have to wait a year to get help, it was some comfort to know it was on its way, at least.

CHAPTER 49

I was helping Mason finish off decorating our bedroom.

"Do you want a drink?" he asked.

I smiled. "Yes—and why are you laughing?"

"You have paint on your face."

I threw a towel at him, missing, as he left the room. I returned to painting but stopped when I heard a noise behind me. I turned around and saw nothing.

"Mason?" I called.

No response. I put the paintbrush down and made my way to the kitchen, still calling Mason's name, still hearing nothing. When I got there, he was lying on the floor. I rushed over to him, but he didn't respond.

I went to phone for help, but someone knocked the phone out of my hands. I looked up and saw a bloody knife in the hands of a masked person. All he did was stare. He went over to Mason, who was still unresponsive, and turned him over. His T-shirt was covered in his blood.

I screamed. The masked figure plunged the knife into my throat, and I gagged for breath as my life slipped away.

* * *

Mason

"Em, wake up!" I shook her hard. The terror on her

face frightened me and I frantically tried to get a response.

Finally, she started to respond. "What happened?" she asked, panicking.

"You woke me up screaming. Are you OK?"

Tears were streaming down her face. "We were painting our room and you offered to make a drink. Next thing I know, you're on the kitchen floor, dead, and the masked figure stabbed me in the throat." She looked confused as she continued. "It felt so real, and the knife in my throat…oh my god, I was choking, I couldn't breathe."

She was losing it again. "Em, focus on me," I said calmly. "You are here with me, so breathe slowly."

I'd never seen her like this before and I have to admit I was worried.

* * *

Emily

I went to the bathroom and threw up. The nightmare had felt so real—in fact, I would have bet that it was. In the mirror, I saw the state I was in and felt ashamed. I knew this phobia wasn't my fault, but I was a grown woman and I shouldn't have behaved like this—it wasn't logical to be scared of masks and Halloween—but here I was, crying and throwing up due to the panic and anxiety.

Mason knocked on the door, but didn't wait for an answer before walking in. He leaned against the sink.

"Em, are you pregnant?"

I shot to my feet as I wiped my mouth. "What…? No, I'm not. I'm being sick because of the way some of the nightmares and masks make me feel."

He looked at me suspiciously. "Are you sure?"

"These attacks make me feel sick. I guess today my body decided enough was enough and so I threw up."

"If you're sure." When I growled at him, he back-pedalled slightly. "OK—sorry I brought it up. I'll get you some water."

I started to wash my face, and when I looked in the mirror, the figure was there. I froze to the spot. A knife appeared in the mirror.

"The more you fear, the stronger I become," the voice said. "Just remember—when you close your eyes, I will be waiting. I'd say have pleasant dreams, but instead I'll say have a frightful nightmare."

"Control your thoughts." I started to talk to myself, saying with each breath, "Don't let this win. I can do this."

"You can try," the voice spat back. "But we both know I'm here to stay, so just get squeamish and have terrible nightmares."

"Go away!" I shouted in the mirror.

"No. And see you soon."

When Mason came back with the water, he found me curled up in a ball on the floor.

"I heard you shouting…"

"That voice is back, and I know it's not real, but why does it bother me?"

"Your fear is ruling you—maybe your imagination is in overdrive and that's where the voice is coming from."

"Don't listen to him," the voice stated. "He is lying."

The more Mason tried to reassure me, the angrier the voice became.

CHAPTER 50

It was Halloween and all my senses were on high alert. Getting through this was going to take a lot of effort. All I had to do was get to the end of the day, then it would be all over. Mason had to go to work and Mark was away for the weekend. Being on my own on a day like today was terrifying. Every noise in the house made me jump. Several times, I checked the doors and windows were locked. I must have looked at the clock a hundred times to see when Mason would be home.

When I turned on the TV, I was very careful about what I watched. However, when I turned to the movie channel, there it was—the top movie to watch was *Halloween*. My body began to tremble; I started feeling sick again. The movie thumbnail wasn't of a mask but of a girl with a knife in her hands. I'd seen enough of those in my dreams, or should I say nightmares. As my hands shook, I managed to skip past it and headed straight for the comedy section.

I'd started to scroll through the comedies when there was a knock at the door. I looked towards it and panicked. I didn't want to open it in case a mask was on the other side, so I approached slowly and shouted, "Who is it?"

"I have a parcel for Mason Gill."

I cautiously opened the door and took the package before quickly locking the door. I left it in the hallway and went back to the TV. I was starting to relax when I heard a noise.

"Hello?" I shouted out. "Anyone there?"

There was no answer. I was on edge; it was frightening. My heart was in my mouth and flashes of fever and chill flashed over me with every step. Every room I went in, I panicked at the thought of what might be waiting for me, but each room was the way I'd left it.

I had just finished looking over the entire house when the key sounded in the lock. I froze, my heart racing.

Then I heard Mason shout, "Hi, it's me."

I started to breathe again and went to greet him. "Thank God you're home."

He looked worried. "Are you OK?"

"I was starting to watch a film to keep my mind occupied when I heard noises and started to freak out. Then the doorbell went, and that didn't help either. What did you order?"

"Just a pair of trainers."

Mason showed me as the doorbell rang. I went into the living room and closed the door. Mason answered, and then came those dreaded words: "Trick or treat." I heard Mason say they looked great but he hadn't gotten anything in.

He opened the door and found me hiding behind it, curled in a ball.

"How about we order pizza and watch the movie in the bedroom?" he said sweetly.

I nodded and quickly made my way up the stairs, shutting the door behind me. Then I rang Mason.

"Can you turn off all the lights so people think we're out?"

"You'll hear the doorbell, as I've ordered pizza, but once it's been delivered, I'll turn out all the lights as I come upstairs."

Twenty minutes later, he came upstairs with the pizza and drinks. All the lights were off and we settled down to watch the movie.

"Thanks for doing this," I said.

"At first, I thought you were nuts, but seeing how it affects you firsthand, if this is what it takes to keep you sane then I'm in. Besides, when have you known me to turn down a takeaway?"

I was getting comfortable when the doorbell went again and I jumped. Mason pulled me close.

"It's just trick-or-treaters," he said. "They'll go away in a minute, so don't worry."

"But they could be…"

"Dressed up… Yes, that's possible, but you can't see them, so don't worry about it."

He was right, but my anxiety levels were high. I focussed on the movie and my food until the day was over. The doorbell didn't go again and, as the night wore on, my anxiety started to return to normal. Hiding in the bedroom wasn't something I'd planned, but it had worked. In fact, locking myself away had meant I kept my Halloween experiences to a minimum. Even though I'd had a few spells, I took comfort in knowing I was free for another year.

CHAPTER 51

First of November and I felt great; it was as if someone had lifted a weight off my shoulders. I was relaxed and for once I looked forward to work, which was unusual. Working in a call centre paid well, but I wouldn't say it was a dream job. I was expected to take call after call and there were times when I started to dread that beep in my ear, as it meant having to deal with another customer. However, after the last few weeks, work would be a welcome change and just the right distraction I needed.

I met Nancy outside the building and we headed to the fag shed to get ready for the day ahead. She had tied her black hair back and wore casual clothes. She was a little overweight, but she'd started a diet because she'd had a baby six months earlier. Once she'd said to me that work was her break and she wanted to talk about everyday things, rather than just babies.

As we headed inside, we were chatting about men and her children when I noticed all the decorations were still up. I froze to the spot. Everything was still the same. Despite what they'd promised me, they weren't taking my condition seriously. My anxiety levels started to rise and I felt sick. I could feel my body shaking and I began to cry. Deep down, I knew nothing would hurt me and it was all in my head, but the overwhelming sense of panic was indescribable. I wanted to run and hide. To think—this morning,

I'd felt wonderful and wanted to come into work!

I bolted to the bathroom. I locked myself in the cubicle and started to retch. I wanted to be sick, but my body would only let me retch. *Let me be sick*, I willed. *Then I might feel better.*

A few minutes later, Nancy called my name and I appeared from the cubicle.

"Emily, are you alright?"

I shook my head. "I feel sick—I can't go back out there. Everyone must think I'm crazy."

She gave half a smile. "You are crazy, but so am I. You don't look good."

"Leo isn't going to like this."

"Who fucking cares what he thinks? You told him about this, so it's not as if it's something new."

"I can't stop shaking…"

"Do you think you can come out and speak to him?"

I looked at Nancy flatly. "I'll have to try, as he can't come in the ladies' bathroom."

I was terrified of going back out there, but I did, taking a deep breath before the bathroom door. Leo was waiting and led me to one of the offices.

"Are you OK?" he asked calmly.

I looked at him with disbelief. "I told you about this phobia and you said that I could have the time off and all decorations would be down before I returned. However, here we are, and they are still up!"

"I said we would try, but we are running a business—"

"Halloween is not part of the business. It's a yearly event, same as Christmas and Easter."

"True, but these are fun events to help all our colleagues relax at work and we can't change everything for just one person."

"It is not about changing everything for me. I

just wanted the decorations down before I came into work so I didn't freak out."

"Well, they're taking the decorations down now, so if you give it thirty minutes then you can log on and start taking calls."

What I was hearing from my team leader's mouth was unbelievable. He expected me to just carry on like nothing had happened. I was on edge, still had heightened anxiety and felt sick, and he wanted me to work in thirty minutes! I couldn't do it.

I tried to stay as calm as possible. "I can't take calls in thirty minutes—I feel sick and I'm panicking."

"I understand, but if you go home, it will be put down as a sickness and, depending on your percentage, you may need an investigatory meeting."

By now, I was sure this wasn't being taken seriously. It felt like I was being bullied to stay at work—or face the consequences.

I took a deep breath, and even though I was shaking, replied, "Leo, I need to go home and calm down."

"Then let me know when you'll be coming back." He was about to leave the room when he turned back to add, "Don't forget to ring in and let HR know that you won't be in today."

He left. They seriously wanted me to ring in. Because they'd forgotten to take the decorations down, they wanted me to feel guilty. As I walked out of the building, I called HR.

CHAPTER 52

I sat in the living room with a drink in hand. As I stared at my drink, I realised I was still shaking. I put the drink down to take deep breaths and close my eyes.

I jumped when I heard the front door.

"Em, why aren't you in work?" I heard Mason say.

I turned to face him, ignoring his question. "Didn't you get my text?" I asked.

"No. Why? What happened?"

"The decorations were still up and I freaked out. My team leader thought I could calm down in thirty minutes and then start taking calls again! Why don't they understand?"

He sat beside me. "This isn't a regular thing," he said softly. "And what I mean by that is it's unusual, so it's new to them. When you explain it in more detail, maybe there will be a better understanding."

It sounded reasonable, but I wasn't sure work would be quite so understanding.

"Hopefully they will, but I'm just trying to calm myself down."

Mason smiled at me. "I know what will help…" he said cheekily. "Making me lunch."

I glared at him but it didn't last long. I gave a smile and said, "Is this your way of killing two birds with one stone? Take my mind off that and fill your stomach?"

"Well, yes—and this way my stomach stops

growling," he said, and kissed me on the cheek.

I was making us both sandwiches when my phone vibrated with a text from Nancy: *Leo is pissed. Watching him pull the decorations down along with the other TLs and they aren't happy. I think an ops manager had words but not in a good way. Will phone later after work.* I texted back: *Thanks for the heads up. Speak later.*

When the food was ready, I called Mason. We sat down and I told him about Nancy's text.

"Why would the operations manager have words with the team leaders?" he asked.

I took a bite of my sandwich before replying. "I don't think she was being nice about the whole thing, but I'll check the details when Nancy calls."

"I get this is new to them, but the decorations would have to come down eventually anyway. Why snap at the team leaders?"

"This is Carol for you. One minute she's calm and the next she's on the warpath. This is all speculation though. I won't really know what's gone on until I talk to Nancy."

Mason didn't look happy, but until we had all the facts he dropped the subject and finished his lunch.

* * *

I was tidying the bedroom when Nancy rang. I was pleased.

"Hi, Nancy. So what happened after I left?"

"Hi, but before I answer—how are you feeling?"

"I'm a lot better, but what happened?" I sat on the bed and made myself comfortable. This was going to be a long conversation.

"Right… After you left Leo started moaning about why you couldn't stay in work to another team leader—"

I interrupted. "Which TL?"

"Don't know the guy's name, but he's a new TL. Anyway, Leo was on one, and in the end, I had to say something…"

"Oh no… What did you say?"

"I told Leo, how would you be if you were scared of something—you know, have a phobia?"

"What did he say?"

"He didn't say anything, but the newbie piped up and said, 'So the decorations were up. She could have stayed in work while they were being pulled down and then gone back to work. She would have had to make the time back for the time missed off the phones.' At this point, I interrupted him and added, 'She's in a state that you can't even imagine and you want to add to her anxiety and tell her she won't get paid for the thirty minutes or the hour she's missed? She was told the decorations would be down before she walked into work, but you want to make out as if it's her fault and not yours'."

"What the hell…"

"Yep, and I could not believe their attitude. Then to top it off, Carol comes over and not only agrees with them, but says you shouldn't be off sick."

My heart sank. I knew work thought I was mad, but to say this in earshot of the floor…

"Fuck's sake… They think that? I can't believe it. But then, at the same time, I'm not surprised, Nancy. Nothing in that place surprises me anymore."

We chatted a bit more on what was going on in our lives, and then she said, "Will you be in tomorrow?"

"Tomorrow is my day off, but hopefully I'll be in the following day and let's hope they'll be a bit more understanding."

CHAPTER 53

I sat in the naughty chair—that's the nickname for when you wait for a team leader to come and get you after being off sick. I looked at my watch. I could have taken a few calls by now. Suddenly, someone calling my name brought me out of my thoughts. I looked up. A woman stood in front of me.

"Are you Emily Brown?" she said.

I nodded, and answered with a smile, "That's right. And you are?"

"I'm Sam and I'm doing your return to work today. One question I have to ask before we go any further: are you OK to return to work?"

"Are the decorations down?" I asked bluntly.

The team leader looked at me, puzzled. "If you're asking about Halloween, then I think they are down—why?"

I shook my head. "Just asking," I said as I followed her to the breakout area.

She smiled at me and said, "I'll do the return to work and take the reason for the absence, then I will give this to HR. Then your team leader will let you know if this is going to be an investigatory meeting in regards to your absences. Do you understand?"

I nodded and let her continue.

"You were off two days..."

"No, I was off one day. Yesterday was my day off anyway."

"Oh, right. I'll make a note and HR can check

that. What was the reason for the absence?"

This will be good, I thought. *When I tell her, I'll get that look of shock and 'what did you just say?'*

"Samhainophobia."

There it was, that look of shock. If I wasn't so serious, I would have burst out laughing at her expression. Clearly, she didn't know what to say, so instead she stayed serious and replied, "Can you repeat that and spell it?"

I took a deep breath and repeated the 'illness' before proceeding to spell the word.

Then came that question. "Can I ask what that is?"

"Samhainophobia is a phobia—fear of Halloween. That's why I asked earlier if the decorations were down."

All this team leader could say in response was, "Oh, OK. Now, if you can sign the return to work, I'll get this off to HR and you can log on."

I smiled politely. "Thanks. Bye."

I returned to my computer, turned it on and waited for it to load. After five minutes, I went to get a drink from the machine. When I got back to my desk, Leo approached me.

"How are you feeling?" he said.

"OK, thanks. Did you want a word?"

"No—just glad to see you are back in work. When I know what the outcome of your percentage is, then I'll let you know."

"Thanks," I replied, smiling.

I was sat at my desk when Nancy arrived.

"Running late?" I asked.

"Kids aren't well, but my mum is looking after them so I can come into work."

"Hope they are better soon. And thanks for letting me know what was going on."

"No problem. Are you having a sick meeting?"

"Don't know yet, but knowing how my luck runs at the moment, more than likely."

Then Leo shouted to the team, "We have customers waiting in the queues, so everyone on calls now please."

Nancy and I looked at each other, rolled our eyes, then started to take calls. After an hour of being bombarded with calls, Leo stood behind me and mouthed 'go into code'. I nodded and, once the call was finished, I went into code and made my way to his desk. I sat opposite him and waited as he finished sending an email.

He turned to me. "HR got back to me and your percentage is over three percent. Three point two, to be exact, so we will need to hold a sick meeting. You can have a union rep with you if you want. We can hold the meeting this afternoon at midday. Is that OK?"

I wasn't surprised. "That's fine. Is it OK if I go and find a union rep?"

"That's fine, just stay in code and get the rep. If there are any problems, then let me know."

"I will do, and thanks."

At least I'd be off the phones for a bit.

I went around the office and found a union rep by the name of Michael. I asked him if he could be present at the meeting and he said midday was fine with him and we'd meet ten minutes before the meeting.

I smiled. "We may need more than ten minutes," I said politely, "as this meeting is based on something different."

He looked intrigued. "Something new? Thirty minutes before, then?"

"That should be fine."

CHAPTER 54

I met Michael in the breakout area and he asked me to explain what was going on. I told him about going home sick a few months ago and again the other day due to the Halloween decorations not being taken down, and about my Samhainophobia. He asked a few questions about the phobia and then said, "Let's see what they have to say before we say anything."

I agreed, then Leo called us into the meeting room.

"This is Alice, and she will be taking the notes for this meeting."

She was another team leader I had seen around the centre. She was always smartly dressed, her hair was never out of place, and she always wore heels to boost her height. She smiled at me but didn't say a word as she got her pen and paper ready for the meeting.

Michael and I took our seats and waited for Leo to start the meeting. He went through the formalities—'Why you are in this meeting?' and 'You have a union rep' and 'Any questions before we start?' As the meeting got under way, Alice and Michael stayed silent, but they both wrote their own notes on the meeting.

"You came in, saw the decorations up and went home due to this phobia."

"Yes, and it's called Samhainophobia. A fear of Halloween. It includes spiderwebs, masks, pumpkins and anything that can come under this heading—however, I'm fine with clowns."

"How long have you known about this fear?"

"The mask fear, I've known since childhood. Halloween, I've never liked, but I'd never thought much about it until recently."

"However, last year you went home after you came into work," Leo stated.

"Carol saw the look on my face and sent me home."

"We had discussed about Halloween," Leo stated again, "and when I spoke to HR, they agreed to book the day off as a holiday."

"Yes, and that was why I took a few days off, so not to spoil anyone else's fun."

"You arranged the few days. They weren't available, but we let you have them anyway."

I ignored the comment because he was trying to make out that they'd done me a favour. I had booked the time off as holidays—there was no favour. Regardless, I let him continue.

"Last year, the decorations were up, and you were still in work prior to Halloween."

I tried my best to explain, hoping I could get through to my team leader. "When people wore their costumes with masks and the dark and gloomy decorations were around, it triggered a severe panic attack and a fear that I'd never had before. Four hundred masks coming from all directions, along with the decorations, made my fear a reality. I'd never put the two together until that day. I had an overwhelming sense of fear and if I had not got out of the building then it could have been worse. That was why this year, I booked time off, so I wouldn't spoil everyone's fun."

"I get that, but the decorations were taken down and you could have returned to work."

"Sadly, the damage was already done. My emotions were off the chart and the panic had set in. Can't just switch it off and return to work."

"Then can you help me understand? I mean, Halloween is a commercial thing, so how do you deal with it?"

"This is new to me, but now I cross the road to avoid shops with decorations in them. I won't go in shops if decorations or costumes are by the door, as I feel sick. If I can go in a shop, then I'll avoid the aisle with Halloween stuff in it."

"Going back to the decorations being up last year. You were in work a few days before Halloween and they were up."

"I felt sick—my stomach was churning—but I never made the connection until Halloween day when people were dressed up."

At this point, I felt like I was repeating myself. I looked at Michael and he nodded reassuringly as if to say *keep going—you are doing OK*.

"I want to understand so I can help support you. Halloween was over the weekend and there were lots of calls—that was why the decorations were still up, because we couldn't spare anyone to take them down. However, when we saw the effect it had on you, we started taking them down."

Team leaders didn't take calls, so they could have taken the decorations down, if they hadn't been too busy chatting rather than working.

My union rep finally spoke. "I think we now understand a bit better. We saw what happened last year."

"Last year it was about the masks," Leo replied flatly.

I wanted to scream, but I stayed calm while Michael added, "Now we know, I think the decorations could have been taken down before

Emily entered the office. Emily feels more could have been done. Could she give you a call before she enters the building?"

Leo seemed to dodge the question and adjourned the meeting. He went straight to HR to see what their take on this was. After ten minutes, he returned to his seat.

"Spoke to HR about what the next steps should be," he said. "It will have to be down as a sick day."

"It shouldn't be a sick day as this was not my fault." I was getting angry now.

Michael added, "This could have been handled better from both sides."

"If you go home," Leo said, "then it will be put down as a sick day. Now we need to take a break so I can check a few things with HR again. We will come back shortly."

* * *

In the break area, I was so angry. Michael was doing his best to keep me calm.

"Emily, I know you're not happy—"

"I feel like they aren't listening to me. I'm trying to be honest with them and it seems to go in one ear and out the other."

"They could use common sense…"

"Yes, they will follow red tape, and I'm starting to think nothing will change."

"You may be able to take this further, but see what they say first. They may surprise you."

"I doubt that. I'll listen first but can't promise anything at the moment."

Leo appeared and said, "We are ready to start the meeting."

We returned to the room, but I really wasn't holding out much hope.

"Are you alright for the meeting to continue?" Leo asked.

"Yes," was all I could say without getting angry.

"The point of this meeting is support, and not to lay blame or fault. It is a learning step, as this is all new. So, we will arrange time off before and after Halloween. Also, you are to ring me before entering the building to check the decorations are down. This isn't a next step, but have you thought about getting help?"

"I am on the waiting list to see someone."

"Good. This will not be a mitigating circumstance, but a sick day, as decided by HR."

"So you're blaming me for taking the day off?"

"No, but you went home instead of staying in work."

It was a relief to hear they'd let me have time off in the future, but I still wasn't happy. "It should not be down as a sick day as it was not my fault."

"You went home, so it's a sick day."

Now I was angry. "If this is the way you want it to be, I will be seeking legal action."

CHAPTER 55

After the meeting, I sat down with Michael.

"Are you OK?" he asked.

Shaking, I replied, "I'm angry. They knew about this because of last year, and now they're blaming me for going home."

"I understand what you are saying, but look at it this way: they now have all the information and they want to help, moving forward."

I looked at Michael as he cleaned his glasses and repositioned them on his face. "I'm still going to see what a solicitor says about this."

"If you still want to speak to them, then that's fine. However, there may be another way than the legal route at this point."

"Like?"

"You could fill out a grievance form if you are not happy and tackle it that way."

I was curious. "How will that help?"

"If you take out a grievance, you'll need to state your reason for doing so, and then it will be addressed by the appropriate person—the operations manager, for example. A solicitor would ask you to try this route before seeking legal action."

I had to admit, he did seem to make sense.

"Can you get this grievance form? I'll fill it out."

* * *

I took the form home with me and, for a long time,

just stared at the blank piece of paper. I had to make this sound good so they could understand. I wrote several drafts just to get the wording right; I wanted this to be taken seriously.

Under the subheading of 'Health and Safety', I wrote:

The company were aware of my fear of masks and Halloween. Due to this, I had to go home, and this should not have been put down as a sick day. Last year, as the decorations were up, I had to take an emergency holiday as I suffered a panic attack. However, I am happy with the next steps provided by my Team Leader. The condition is known as Samhainophobia.

Once that was done, I could relax for the rest of the evening. Mason was working until the early hours due to stock-taking, so I welcomed having the place to myself.

While I was making food, I heard a bang. I stopped and went to investigate, but I found nothing. I returned to making my dinner, but I heard the noise again.

The voice mocked me. "Other people don't know you like I do. I'm always here, just be fearful and I'll appear."

Just what I needed—work and this thing taking the piss out of me.

CHAPTER 56

When I arrived at work, I met up with Michael and handed him the grievance form.

He looked it over. "Straight to the point. Do you want to add anything?"

"I can't think of anything to add. I just want this handed in."

Michael smiled at me. "I'll hand it in to HR for you now."

"Thank you."

After that, I carried on with my day as normal. When I looked at the clock, there was only half an hour of work left. The day had gone surprisingly fast, but I was still grateful to be going home soon. Suddenly, Leo appeared out of nowhere.

Before I could take another call, he said, "Your grievance can be heard next week on Tuesday at eleven. You can have a union rep with you. Is that date alright with you?"

They were actually taking this seriously. Once the shock wore off, I was pleased and promptly nodded in agreement. "That date is fine. I'll just let my rep know now before I leave."

Leo surprised me by saying, "Log out now and sort things out with your rep."

I didn't argue if it meant time off the phones and quickly left before he changed his mind.

I found Michael and told him the date and time of the grievance.

"I'll clear my calendar so I don't have to rush to another meeting," he said.

"I hope it won't be that long."

"Depends what you have to say and what questions they have to ask."

I had my reservations about the upcoming meeting, because I really didn't see how things were going to change. What was worse, because I was explaining my phobia over and over like a broken record, it was always on my mind. With it, my anxiety and fear wouldn't go away. I couldn't find peace.

The doctor had told me it was a phobia, but the psychiatrist would have to be the one to officially diagnose me. At this point, I doubted they would disagree with the doctor, but for now, it was a waiting game.

* * *

Mason and I were eating when he finally said, "Is something wrong? You've been very quiet since I came in."

I started to play with my hair, twisting it around my finger, as I ignored the question.

"Emily!"

I almost jumped. "Work are hearing my grievance on Tuesday…"

"That's great, Em."

I just stared into his green eyes. "Is it? I just don't think it's going to make any difference."

"Hear them out."

It was exactly the wrong thing to say. "Hear them out—is that all anyone can say? I freaked out last year and had to come home. This year I thought they would understand, after last year, and have the decorations down before I walked in, but no, they didn't. But they expect me to do all the chasing and make sure all the decorations are down. How about they take me seriously and ring me? If Leo isn't in, then they should make sure another TL rings me. Why are they trying to say it's all my fault? I never asked for this. I'm the one waiting for an appointment, and in the meantime living in hell—"

"Stop! Em, calm down. Remember I've seen this firsthand. Hopefully, this time they will take this seriously and it will get sorted. Try and see from their point of view—this is something new for you and them, so it will take time to get sorted."

His little speech just made me angrier. "I see you are standing up for them."

"That's not what I'm saying…"

"Sounds like it."

He went to say more, but I left the room before it turned into a full-blown row.

The rest of the night, we stayed out of each other's way; I watched TV in the bedroom while he stayed in the living room. When he finally came up, he smiled and acted like nothing had happened.

"What have you been watching?" he asked

"Whatever was on the comedy channel."

I didn't even bother asking what he'd been watching because I still wasn't happy after our conversation earlier.

"Do you want a cuppa?" he asked.

Once he'd brought up the tea, we just cuddled up together watching TV.

CHAPTER 57

I sat downstairs, shaking. I had just had the same nightmare—a man with a knife chasing me through the town, catching up to me and killing me. The stress with work and all of the meetings and having to explain myself over and over was not helping. It kept my phobia at the front of my mind, even though Halloween was over until next year.

I went back to bed to find Mason was still fast asleep but had taken up the bed in my absence. As I got into bed, I rolled him over to get more space. I'd thought I'd be able to fall back asleep, but I remained wide awake, staring at the ceiling. I looked at the clock—three in the morning. I had to be up by eight as work was at ten.

I got up and made my way downstairs, only to discover Mark was up.

"You couldn't sleep either, Sis?"

"No, and I really need sleep." I got the milk out of the fridge as Mark made the tea. "Why are you up?"

He handed me a mug. "It's this girl I've been seeing... Well, she dumped me."

I wanted to feel sorry for my brother, but I couldn't—after all, he loved and left them in very quick succession. Then I noticed his eyes were heavy, as if he'd been crying.

"Mark, did you like this one?"

A smile must have crept over my face because he snapped back. "You don't have to look so happy that I'm in pain."

"Oh please, now you finally realise what it's like to be on the end of this relationship roller-coaster. Now, hopefully, the next one you meet might stand a chance, because you won't be out for what you can get."

"Oh, yes, my sister has it all figured out." Mark was angry. "Living with her boyfriend, not engaged... That's right—Mason was going to ask but hasn't yet—"

My head was spinning. "Mason was what? Engagement?"

Suddenly, Mark snapped out of his anger and started to backtrack. "Engaged? Don't know what you're talking about."

I glared at my him. "What do you know, Mark?"

He shook his head. "I don't know anything, and I think it's time I went back to bed."

I went to say something, but he quickly left the room.

* * *

The following morning, I saw my brother in the kitchen. We didn't speak, but he looked very sheepish. He looked tidy and as if he had slept, which always annoyed me as I felt and looked like shit.

Mason walked in and looked at each of us in turn. "Have you two had a fight?"

Mark gave me the same look he used to when our parents interrogated us—*please don't say anything*. However, I wanted to know the truth.

"Mason, were you going to ask me to marry you?"

Mason spat out his drink and looked straight at my brother. "You asshole—I told you to keep quiet."

"What... You *were* going to ask me?"

Mason looked at me and softly said, "I did have a conversation with Mark, but that was it."

"So you don't want to marry me?"

Mason stood, lost for words, a moment too long, eyes alternating between looking at me with wide panic and glaring daggers at my brother. "Em, can we talk about this later as I do have to get to work—"

I interrupted him. "Work is all you can say at a time like this."

Mason shot another look at Mark.

"Sorry, Mase—I didn't mean to—"

"Sorry, the damage is done." Mason turned to me. "Em, it's been on my mind a lot lately, but I really have to get to work."

They both quickly left, leaving me with more questions than answers. Why wasn't he asking? Was he angry with me? And the worst one: was he considering leaving me? All these thoughts because he wouldn't stay and talk about this.

CHAPTER 58

When I arrived home, Mason had already started dinner. He poured me a glass of wine and gave it to me with a kiss.

"Sorry about this morning, but I'd been caught off guard."

Taking a sip of my wine, I let him continue.

"The truth is...before you accused me of trying to kill you, I had been looking at rings. Then you broke up with me..."

"Hun, I didn't mean it," I interjected, putting my glass down.

He put his arms around me. "I know," he said, tone soft, "but I was hurt, angry and confused. After a while, I realised I wasn't prepared to lose you and when we moved in together... Well, that put the asking in the background. Am I making sense?"

I searched his green eyes and they told me he still loved me, but now I knew... I had to admit, I wanted more.

"I think I do, but now I know, I'm upset because you won't ask me."

He cupped my face. "I want to ask, but with what's going on, I don't think it's the right time."

I pulled away from his embrace and placed my hand on my forehead, trying to think of what to say. That was when I turned the tables on him.

I looked at him with a smile. "If you won't, then I will. Mason Gill, will you marry me?"

Shock flashed through his eyes. He'd forgotten

he was cooking and the food was starting to burn.

"What did you say?"

"Well, if I wait for you to ask, then I'll be waiting forever, so what is your answer? Will you marry me?"

"Isn't the man supposed to ask?" The shock in his voice was obvious.

"Well, you haven't or won't, so I've asked twice. So, what's the answer?"

His eyes stayed glued to me, expression caught between impressed and disbelieving. "I guess we're getting married then. You know I haven't got a ring yet, right?"

I smiled. "I know, but finally it's out in the open. We're getting married."

"You know I wanted to ask, right?"

I hugged him. "I know. But since we had that break because of me, and then hearing that you were going to ask... Well, I decided to ask because I didn't want to wait any longer."

He kissed me and said, "I don't want to tell anyone until I've got you a ring."

"Well, you'd better get one soon, because something like this will get out, and if my mum and your mum find out then the whole world will know."

"Don't worry about that. Takeaway alright? Dinner is ruined."

I started to laugh. "Takeaway it is then."

CHAPTER 59

After a few great days, I was in work, waiting outside the office with Michael for my grievance meeting to start. A short time later, a woman appeared.

"Hi, Michael," she said. "If you and Emily are ready then please come through."

She seemed nice enough—medium height and build with blonde short hair.

As Michael and I walked towards the room, he turned to me and said, "That's one of the operation managers here—Helen."

When we sat down, she introduced herself. "Hi, I'm Helen. I am here to take this meeting as an impartial operations manager. This is Kim, who will be taking the notes for today's meeting," she said, gesturing to a woman sat to one side, "and I can see you have Michael as your rep. Are we OK to continue?"

I sat back in the chair and got comfortable as I answered, "Yes."

"This is a grievance hearing, so in line with procedure, there is a checklist to ensure consistency that will enable me to reach a conclusion."

"OK."

Kim was frantically trying to keep up with what we were saying. Whenever these meetings took place, I did feel sorry for the notetaker—their hand must absolutely kill them at the end of each meeting.

I drew my attention back to Helen and what she had to say.

"I will ask some questions and then adjourn to make a decision."

I nodded and repeated, "OK."

"Just so you understand, this is not a disciplinary meeting, and anything you say is confidential, so you need to be honest with me."

"OK." Maybe I should have just put the word 'OK' on tape so I wouldn't have had to repeat the same thing over and over in these meetings.

Then Helen started to ask questions. "Can you state exactly why you've raised this grievance?"

Finally, I had a chance to explain my side of the story. "It is being raised because the company knew of my fear of Halloween when I came in last year and saw four hundred masks. My heart was racing and felt like it would come out of my chest as I raced into the toilets and Carol sent me out of the building. The team leader who brought out my things said that Carol had put it as unauthorised holiday.

"Then, a few months before Halloween this year, I asked what the plans were and was told that the decorations would not go up until I was away. Carol was kind enough to authorise a few days for me. When I came back after the few days, I walked back into the building and saw the decorations still up. Due to last year, the memory of four hundred masks still haunts me, and I ended up having a panic attack. I saw Carol and she told me to take an hour out. I didn't feel that was enough because I couldn't cope. I took the time off so I didn't spoil the fun for everybody else."

"What do you want the outcome of today to be?" Helen asked.

Once she had spoken, I suddenly remembered they'd asked a very similar question in my previous meeting. It was probably a standard line they used. They really were not taking this meeting seriously, but as I had been told by everyone, I'd see how it went. It might surprise me.

I answered the question. "I don't want the absence to be sick. I am willing to take it as unpaid leave."

She thought for a moment and then replied, "Did you have a meeting about your illness?"

"Yes."

"What was the outcome of that meeting?"

"They put it down as a sick day, and they also put in next steps. In future, Leo is to ring me and let me know about the decorations, or I am to ring and check. I have also been advised that I can have time off work during this period."

Helen glanced over at Kim, who was still busy writing the notes. She seemed to be struggling, so before we continued with the meeting I casually told her, "I know I'm talking a lot, but if you need me to slow down so you can catch up, please let me know."

Kim looked up from the notes and smiled. "Thank you for the offer. If I need to, I'll ask you to slow down, but please continue."

"So," Helen said, "an agreement has been put in place?"

"Yes, it has."

"Did you ring at the time?"

"No, as it did not occur to me, although I did hear that upstairs was clear."

She gave a nod. "OK."

Then Michael added his piece to the meeting. "Emily assumed they would be down. Leo said it had been a very busy morning and he knew about Emily's phobia. They did take them down immediately when Emily came in, but the damage was already done."

"So, to clarify, the reason for today's meeting is that you want clearer procedure regarding when an absence is sick pay?"

I was just repeating myself—everything I said went in one ear and out the other—but I had to stay calm and try to make myself heard.

"This is about duty of care. Until I worked here, I didn't know how bad it was. When this first happened, there were masks walking around, and when I walked in with the decorations up, it brought it all back. The doctors are sending me to a psychiatrist to help with this."

Helen gave the appearance that she was listening but, as the meeting continued, it felt very pointless.

"Going forward, the next steps will support you?"

"For next year, yes, but not this year. The holidays were helpful, but when I came back to work, I didn't expect to walk in and have it happen all over again. I don't feel the company is trying to help, because I just walked into my fear all over again."

At this point, Michael added more to the meeting, in the hopes that they would be more helpful. "The company has been very supportive by giving holidays. Leo knew that if it hadn't been manic, the decorations would have been down."

Helen then responded to Michael but looked at me. "Part of the responsibility was yours; you could have called in. I understand how this can affect you, but if you had called in, this could have all been avoided."

There it was again—turning it round so they could blame me.

"I have a friend that works on the second floor," I said, "and they had mentioned to me that all the decorations were down. I also have since learnt that, if I had called Leo, he wouldn't have been in that early so he would not have known and, as I said, I didn't think to ring in because we were in November. Also, they did say the decorations would have been taken down before I returned."

"So just to clarify, this meeting is about the process?"

"Yes, it's about health and safety, a duty of care."

Helen nodded. "So is there anything else?"

I thought for a moment before replying. "No—I don't think so."

Michael added, "Emily agrees with, and will fully comply with, the next steps in the future."

Helen quickly glanced at Kim, who was still writing, and said, "I will now adjourn and we will reconvene this afternoon. Is two o'clock OK?"

"Yes."

I came out of the meeting feeling that I wasn't being taken seriously and that I was to blame for all this. I went for my break and then back on the phones until it was time for the next stage of the meeting.

When the meeting reconvened again, we took our places at the table.

"I have looked through the file again to gain an overall picture," Helen said. "Last year was about not liking Halloween, and yet this year you have said you have a condition."

I wanted to bang my head on the table— everything I was saying was on repeat—but instead I smiled. "I haven't been officially diagnosed yet as I am still waiting to see the psychiatrist. However, the doctors believe the condition is a phobia."

"When you discussed this with Carol and the emergency holiday was agreed, this was the first occasion. This year, we arranged holidays for you and, when you returned, you were not fit to be here. Therefore, it was an unplanned absence, and in this case, the process was to record this as an absence as it was a sickness. Do you understand the difference between last year and this year?"

I knew what was coming but answered, "Yes."

"Just a thought," Michael said. "Emily feels that the company is at fault due to the decorations not being removed."

Helen responded by saying, "Earlier, you said you wanted the absence to be overturned, but as this is process, I cannot remove the sick day." I was getting the impression she didn't like Michael adding to the meeting.

"OK."

"The only other points stated on the grievance were around the sick day."

"Yes."

Then Helen went through the grievance point by point. "The grievance is centred around the absence and I cannot overturn the absence and make it into a holiday. Another point is that a phone call would have been nice. I accept that; however, part of the responsibility was yours to contact us. In the future, you have next steps to follow."

Michael didn't seem happy with the way the meeting was going. "Yes, however, Emily says the company had a duty of care to ensure they were all down."

After he had spoken, I added, "I understand that, but I didn't want to spoil anyone else's fun. I did take precautionary measures."

Helen then asked, "What would you like to get out of today?"

"I believe my absence should be overturned on health and safety grounds."

"I cannot overturn the process—if a person is unfit to work, it has to be a sick day."

I needed to stress the point. "I was well enough to be in work, but when I came in and saw the decorations up, I then became unwell."

"We have discussed that you didn't feel well enough to stay. The absence is not mitigating, so we made the choice to issue next steps to support you. They have been issued, but you need to take part of that responsibility. Going forward, the next steps will be followed next year so things will happen differently."

I really wanted to believe her, but my doubts still remained as she continued, "What I will do is reinforce all that has been said. We will need to be mindful and keep you informed."

Then the meeting was ended. Through the entire meeting, I had not been taken seriously, and I doubted things would change within the work environment, no matter how much I wanted to believe them.

CHAPTER 60

When I finished climbing the stairs to my floor, I opened the door and no one else was there. As I made my way to my desk, I didn't pay too much attention to the fact I was there on my own until I saw the time on the clock. It was eleven o'clock and it was still dark outside. When I looked around the office again, all the Halloween decorations were still up. I put my bag down and started to walk down the aisle towards the breakout area. Something didn't feel right, so I called out. No one answered.

When I got to the breakout area, it was clear of decorations. I started to breathe a little easier but I still felt uneasy. I tried to control my breathing so I could think more clearly, but it wasn't working.

My eyes went to the stairwell—a way out. I opened the door and heard a noise. I should have listened to my instincts and just carried on through the door, but I didn't. I turned back and called out again, but still no one answered.

I wanted my bag, but it was in the office area with the decorations. I felt trapped in the breakout area, as either section of the office was just as terrifying.

Then I heard a noise again. This time, when I turned around, a man with a mask was standing there looking at me. A knife was in his hand. I stumbled backwards and that was when he started to come towards me. Due to the mask he wore, I couldn't see his face, and I wasn't going to stick around to find out.

I ran back towards the stairwell, but he stepped in front of the doors, blocking my way. I had no choice but to go through the office with the decorations. I was now in flight mode—I wanted out of this nightmare.

I ran down the aisle. Halfway down the office, I glanced back. He wasn't there. Out the corner of my eye, I saw my bag was still on my desk. I retrieved it and made my way towards the door. Suddenly, the masked man appeared in front of me. I screamed, turning back through the office from hell. When I looked back to see if he was gaining on me, he had disappeared.

I was in the middle of the office floor, my body shaking and tears running down my face. Suddenly, he appeared again, leaning against a wall, twisting the knife in his hand. He touched his finger to the tip of the knife, stopped, looked up at me and started walking towards me again.

I ran the other way. As I turned the corner, he was just standing there, staring at me. As I ran in the other direction, away from him, it dawned on me that I was caught in some loop—it didn't matter which direction I went in, he'd always be one step ahead of me.

"Do you like this game?" the voice said, excited.

I screamed out loud, tears still streaming. "Leave me alone."

Then the voice laughed. "I wish I could, but this is so much fun, don't you think?"

"Just leave me alone!" Even though I was screaming back, my voice was shaken and frightened.

Then I heard that cackling laugh.

When the laughing stopped, the masked man was in front of me. In horror, I watched him raise the knife above me. As it came down, he missed.

He stumbled forward, not anticipating this. He glanced at me, now picking up the pace. I was running for my life around an empty office with no way out. When I glanced back, his mood had changed. He started picking things up from the desks and hurling them in my direction. Each time he missed, the darker he became.

My body was in overdrive. As I ran, I threw up—some ended up on the floor but most went on me. Panic and fear held me captive as I tried desperately to escape, all the while watching him get closer and closer to me.

CHAPTER 61

Sweat dripped off me as I ran. Each time I saw a way out, he blocked the exit. My heart felt like it was going to escape through my chest; my anxiety levels had reached heights I'd never thought possible. I couldn't stop, even for a moment—he was gaining on me. My body was getting tired, but I had to keep going.

As I came to a clearing, I cut through a row of desks, but here, there were more Halloween decorations than anywhere else in the office. There were masks everywhere. My body trembled badly; I knew I had no choice as I heard him coming. I noted where everything was, then shut my eyes and made a run for it. I hit something and hurt my knee. When I opened my eyes, I had run straight into a chair. Now I was in the middle of the masked area. The sweat was running down my face; I was shaken, overrun with panic. I didn't know if I'd get out of this alive.

I tried to pinch myself in the hopes that I would wake up, but nothing happened. Suddenly, breath stroked my neck and a chill went down my spine. I slowly turned around, and there, right in front of me, was the masked man.

Screaming, I stared at him. Even through the mask, I could see no eyes. Where they should have been were black holes. I screamed even louder, stepping backwards, trying to get away. If he had black holes for eyes, did that mean he had no soul?

For each step I took back, he took one forward to keep the gap between us even. I quickened my pace. To my horror, he kept up.

I turned away and started to run, but I heard him running behind me. Then he gripped my arm. When I looked back, he just stared at me, expressionless. I tried to pull away, but his grip was too strong. Using my other hand, I tried to prise his cold fingers from my arm, but nothing worked. I kicked him, but he didn't even flinch—it was like he didn't feel anything—and his cold hand was around my throat, pinning me against the wall. I was forced to look into his black-hole eyes as he held me there. I tried to close my eyes, but his grip tightened until I opened them again.

He ran the knife over my cheek and trickles of blood ran down my face. He showed me the knife, red with my blood, taking pleasure in my pain. As he held me against the wall, I felt a sharp pain across my chest. He showed me the knife, now even bloodier. He was deliberately cutting parts of me, savouring the pain he caused.

He didn't speak but a voice said, "I told you we would meet and this would be fun."

I just wanted this all to be over. If that meant an end to my life, then so be it—I couldn't take any more. If I'd thought this pain was bad, nothing had prepared me for the excruciating pain I felt. Looking down, he'd plunged the knife into my chest, taking pleasure as he twisted it.

Suddenly, the pain stopped. For a moment, he looked into my eyes, never saying a word. It was if he was searching for something, some type of reaction that he wasn't getting. Then I felt that excruciating pain all over again as he twisted the knife inside me.

Abruptly, he let go of me. Because of the pain

and blood loss, I collapsed to the floor. He knelt beside me, just staring at me. He seemed to take real pleasure in my agony. Then I saw the knife in his hand, now covered all in blood, my blood. He held my throat with his free hand, and I had only one thought: he was going to slit my throat and finally put an end to this horror.

CHAPTER 62

I gasped for air as the knife slid across my throat and my life slipped away. The next thing I knew, I was standing over the toilet, throwing up.

Mason came in. "Are you alright? Because you bolted out of bed and ran in here—is there something I need to know?"

I had about a minute before I threw up again, so I quickly turned to Mason and said with sarcasm, "You're off the hook—I'm not pregnant. Now leave me alone."

I turned back before I threw up on the floor.

"Em, I didn't mean it like that…"

I shot him a glare and he left the bathroom.

After I finally finished throwing up, I cleaned myself up and went back to bed. Mason was still awake.

"Are you OK?" he asked sweetly.

I couldn't face him, so kept my back to him. "I've had the nightmare from hell, and then you imply that I'm pregnant."

He stroked my arm. "Do you want to tell me about the nightmare?"

"I was in the office and the decorations were up, and then a masked man chased me around the office with a knife."

"Well, you're safe now."

I bolted upright and looked at him, my anger building, but I tried to stay calm. "Safe… These dreams or nightmares are hell, then work is blaming me instead of helping me, and the images are not only getting clearer, but the nightmares are increasing and not getting better, because between work and Halloween, I'm the one suffering."

I didn't wait for a response before turning back and saying quickly, "Good night."

"Night, Em." Mason tried to hug me, but I pulled away.

* * *

In the morning when Mason came downstairs, I apologised for snapping at him.

He smiled. "It's OK, but I was worried about you."

I had to ask. "You didn't really think I was pregnant, did you?"

"You were throwing up a lot, so it did cross my mind."

"Well, that part of our life is way off." I smiled back at him.

* * *

Over the next few weeks, the nightmares calmed down, and I was happy that my life had returned to normal—well, my normal anyway. Mason bought a ring, and what could I say? It was beautiful. It was shaped like a flower and shone beautifully on my left hand. Now all I needed to top this off was for my brother to move out and Mason and I to have the place to ourselves, but that wouldn't be for a while, unfortunately.

Work was just that—work. Go in, take calls, one after another, and then go home. Things were just uneventful and normal and I loved it.

However, everything was about to change.

Today would leave me not only off balance, but terrified. I didn't see it coming until it was too late.

The weather was sunny and warm, which put everyone in a great mood, including myself, as it felt like summer was just starting. I walked into work with a smile, but when I got to my desk, I had this feeling it was going to be a long day, so I went to the shop to get some snacks for my shift.

Still blissfully unaware that things were about to change, I walked back into the building, carrying my food, and made my way up the stairs. That was when it happened. At the top of the stairs, right in front of me, were masks, loaded on a board. Panic hit me hard. I ran past, my body trembling and shaking. When I reached my desk, the tears had already started and my body was telling me I needed to throw up. Some of my team noticed the state I was in and guided me to the breakout area. Like a child, I rocked back and forth, making no sense as I tried to string a sentence together. It was the worst I'd been since finding out about this phobia.

I wanted to be fine and snap out of this, but I couldn't. In my head, I told myself, *This is stupid— you are a grown woman. Get a grip. This isn't logical, as it makes no sense*. But no matter what I thought, all these feelings were real, and they made my life hell.

As I rocked back and forth, people stared at me while they got drinks and snacks from the machine only inches from where I was sitting. They didn't ask if I was alright—the look on my face must have said that I wasn't, but they all looked puzzled about the why.

A team leader came over to ask what was wrong and my union rep, Michael, appeared. He was on the phone with Mason due to the state

I was in, while the team leader tried to get a coherent sentence out of me.

"Masks...stairs..." was all they could understand.

They asked why I hadn't noticed them when I first came in. I managed to say, in a clearer voice but still in a state, "Lots of people were at the top of the stairs."

They tried to tell me to give myself an hour to calm down and then return to work, but Michael heard them and responded on my behalf, "Emily will need to go home, as she is in no fit state to work. I've contacted her partner and he's on his way to take her home."

I was relieved that someone was fighting my corner, even while the look on the team leader's face showed the lack of empathy and understanding with what was really happening.

CHAPTER 63

Kim took me outside.

"Are you alright?" she asked.

I looked at her in disbelief. "It's summer... Why would they do this?"

"It's to raise money for charity."

All I could think was, *Why use masks? Bake cakes or something…anything but this*, but I asked firmly, "And how does this work?"

She stayed calm and tried to justify why the masks were up. "We wanted to raise money for charity and we thought that people could buy a plain white mask and decorate it. I mean, these aren't horror."

"The plain white masks are horror, and if people can decorate them how they want, then someone may decorate it in a horror style. You know about my fear—you were there in the meeting—and yet no one warned me, and now I have to go home because of this."

Looking me straight in the eye, she answered, "Well, it's your choice to go home. We're prepared to give you a bit of time off the phones to calm down, then you could start taking calls."

I wanted to reply, but Mason arrived to take me home.

"Em, let's get you home," he called through the open window, before turning to Kim and saying, "Thanks for staying with her."

As I got in the car, she smiled at him and then returned to the call centre.

While he drove, Mason asked, "Do you want to say what happened?"

"There were masks at the top of the stairs and I freaked out," I said, looking in my bag for a fag, but they weren't there. Of course they weren't—I'd been trying to cut down, hoping to quit. "Everyone thinks I'm nuts—you should have seen the looks I got. The team leader who waited with me, that was Kim. Well, she implied it was my choice to go home, and said they were willing to give me an hour to calm down. They aren't taking this seriously, and they're making me feel as if this is all my fault."

When we arrived home, Mason made me a cup of tea and sat me down.

"It's not your fault, Em," he said. "I have a friend that works in the call centre—I'll get him to take a picture of the masks so I can see for myself. Now finish the tea I made while I text him."

Mason texted his friend and, an hour later, he said, "He sent me the picture. I won't show you, but now I can see what you saw."

"It's summer, so why would they do this? I used to have some comfort that this only happened at a certain time of year, but now I have to get used to the fact it could happen at any time and affect me like this."

Mason held my hand. "I don't know why—as you said, it's summer—but when you're calmer, you'll need to talk to work and sort this out."

"I've tried a few times, and each time they say they have a better understanding and they will warn me and so on... Well, where was the warning here? No, they just let me go into work and let me get frightened all over again, and then they say, 'Take an hour and get back to work'.

They give the impression it's all me and I can manage this and that they aren't responsible."

Suddenly, my phone rang. When I answered, it was Michael.

"Hi," he said. "I know it's a stupid question, but how are you feeling?"

"Terrible, and I can't believe they have done this."

Mason wanted to know who was on the line, so I covered the mouthpiece and told him, "It's Michael, my union rep, who you spoke to."

Then I listened to Michael as he continued.

"They're taking the masks down from the stairwell, but they are going to continue with the masks to raise money. I thought I'd let you know."

My head was spinning. "Thanks, Michael, for telling me. Now, the time off I take—they'll blame me again. What can I do?"

After a moment's pause, he replied, "You could take out another grievance, but this time against the individuals. There were enough people that knew about this and have not followed their own next steps in order to prevent this."

I thought for a moment before answering. "I won't be back tomorrow. Can you get the form for me, please? I'll get Mason to collect it from you."

"I'll make sure the form is ready, just let me know when. And just remember to ring in so they know you won't be in tomorrow."

CHAPTER 64

Mason picked up the new grievance form. I looked at it and thought long and hard about what I was going to say, before I put the words on paper.

This grievance is against Carol, Helen, Leo, Kim and Alice. They all have firsthand knowledge of my phobia of masks, due to previous meetings. Next steps that were laid down by them meant that I would be informed if there were to be any masks within the building, but no one followed the next steps. This caused me to have a panic attack and prevented me from attending work.

So HR had more information, I then wrote what seemed like an essay about why I was bringing another grievance. I explained that these people had been in either one or more of the meetings, and so they knew how this phobia affected me. I also said that I'd had a day off, so hadn't been aware that these masks would be up on display. I gave details of the meetings and of the next steps that had been put in place, and I finished by saying that my trust in the company had been damaged. I also said I was at the point where I was afraid to come into work, because every meeting had led to nothing more than an 'it will be OK'.

* * *

Mason was making a drink when I walked into the kitchen.

"Did you give the form to Michael?"

He took a sip of his drink. "Yes, I did. We spoke briefly and he said to tell you 'get better soon', and he'll see you when you get back.'"

"That's sweet of him, and thank you."

He came over and kissed me. "That's OK, but now I have to go to work. I have a feeling I won't finish on time, so don't wait till I get in to have food."

Sometimes it felt like he was married to the store, but then, being store manager gave him some flexibility to deal with my situation. I returned his kiss and watched until he left the house.

I had just sat down when my phone rang. I'd left it in the kitchen when I'd been speaking to Mason and I reached it just in time before it rang out.

When I answered, it was Leo.

"Hi, Emily. How are you today?"

I took a seat in the kitchen and answered him. "I'm doing alright. How can I help?"

There was a lot of noise in the background—he was in the call centre, and it was business as usual.

"I'm just ringing to let you know that the charity event is going on till the end of the week, but we feel that you could still come to work."

I was stunned. "And how is this going to work?" I snapped back.

"It has been suggested that maybe you could work in-store."

I couldn't believe what I was hearing. They had done wrong by not following their own next steps, and yet here they were, giving me suggestions on where to work so they could feel guilt-free.

"I work in the office; why should I have to go into store just because you're running a charity event? And when I say you, I don't mean you personally, before you try and twist that."

"I know what you meant, Emily. It's just, rather than take the time off unpaid, this is what's been suggested, and to be honest, I think it's not a bad idea."

Obviously, Leo had no idea that I'd handed in the grievance against him. He wouldn't be making this suggestion if he did.

The conversation went back and forth for a while longer, until I made my feelings about working elsewhere, other than the centre, very clear. When the phone call ended, I phoned the doctor so I could be signed off sick until this so-called charity event was over. They were trying to palm me off so they could feel guilt-free and say that they had found an alternative solution to my problems.

CHAPTER 65

The doctor gave me a sick note for a week, which Mason handed in for me. I'd like to say I enjoyed my time off, especially because it was the summer, but I'd be lying. I hated it.

During this week, Leo kept in contact, but I could tell he'd been informed about the grievance against him and the other members of staff because he was very careful about what he said to me over the phone. He did, however, inform me that by the time I was due back, all the masks would be down, and that there would be a walk-through before I returned to work. This meant there was no risk that I'd have to extend my absence.

I still could not understand why they'd allowed the masks to be up. I appreciated that charities need money, but they knew they had someone with a phobia of masks—who now needed to take a week off work. Surely, they could have picked something different to raise money?

Later that day, Mason phoned and told me he would be working till the early hours of the morning due to everything going wrong at the store. And if that wasn't bad enough, he also told me that he'd be leaving the next day to attend a conference and he'd be staying overnight. I tried to argue the point, but as Mason pointed out, being the store manager has its perks but also its downsides, and this was one of them.

However, I still tried to change his mind. "Can't you just tell them to get lost?"

"Em, I know you don't like this, but it's part of my job."

"Well, I don't want you to go away."

"You're being unreasonable now and sounding childish," Mason replied, his voice becoming firm. "This is part of my job; I've been the store manager as long as we've been dating and this is the first time I've had to go away. We can talk about this more when I get home but, as I said, everything that could go wrong has gone wrong, and I need to go. Talk to you later."

And with that, he hung up.

I looked at my phone in disbelief. I hadn't expected our conversation to end so abruptly. It wasn't fair that he loved his job so much, while I was trapped in a job I'd started to hate because of all the tension.

I was starting to think about food when Michael rang.

"Hi, Emily," he said. "I thought I would give you a ring because I've spoken to HR and they've given me a date for your grievance to be heard. They want to do this meeting next Wednesday, if that's OK with you?"

I thought for a moment. "That's the day I return to work after being off for the week, so that will be fine. I just want to get this meeting out of the way."

"I know what you mean. The people that you have named in the grievance have been told they are not to contact you to discuss the matter or to discuss it between themselves, but that one is going to be difficult to control."

"To be honest, Michael, it wouldn't surprise me if they discussed it between themselves. Nothing surprises me anymore when it comes to that centre. I just wish they could understand and follow their own next steps."

The phone conversation continued for a while longer. It was nice to hear someone sympathise with the situation, rather than blame me. Michael let me know it was going to be a long meeting, and all I needed to do was give them the facts and help them understand what it meant to experience this phobia in the hopes it would change their mind.

Just before we ended the call, he asked, "Have you heard about the appointment yet?"

"If you mean about the psychiatrist, not yet. I'm still waiting, but I wish they would hurry up."

"If they ask, you can tell them in the meeting that you haven't heard from them. However, if you do hear anything, then in the meeting you can update them."

"I'll let you know if I hear anything. In fact, I'll chase up the doctors and find out. Then I'll let you know when I see you on Wednesday."

When I did phone the surgery, it was as I'd expected: they hadn't had a response and were still waiting, but if they didn't hear anything by the end of the week then they would chase the department and get back to me.

CHAPTER 66

My week off went so fast, and suddenly, I was back at work, dreading the meeting later on that morning. Michael found me as I logged in.

"You may as well go into code as you won't be taking calls yet," he said with a smile.

I smiled back. "OK."

I put the code into the phone and went with him to the breakout area.

We discussed how I should approach this meeting, giving them the facts and telling them how this phobia made me feel. I also raised concerns that I didn't think this meeting was going to change anything, as nothing had changed after the others.

Suddenly, a woman approached us. I recognised her from around the building but didn't know her personally. She was dressed tidily and had a slim build with bobbed brown hair.

"Hi, Michael," she said. "We are ready when you are."

We watched as she disappeared back into a room, and then Michael turned to me.

"She's one of the better ones. It's a pity she's not conducting this meeting."

"Do you mean she actually has a heart?"

He smiled at me. "If you want to put it like that—yes, she does. Grace is the type of team leader that will listen to a person and care about what they have to say. She conducts meetings and her team with time and respect, and there aren't many of them in this building that will do that."

When we entered the room, we sat down in front of another manager, who introduced himself as Derek before introducing Grace as the notetaker. He was tall and slim and came across as very friendly as we started the meeting. He asked the usual questions: "Are you alright? This is an investigation meeting, so please be honest with me, so I can get a better picture of what is going on."

It was nothing I hadn't heard before in the other meetings, so I was very sceptical. My trust in this call centre had been badly damaged.

Derek told me that he would look at the facts and interview the other people involved and then decide what the outcome would be. Again, all the same as before. He also said that if I needed a break at any point, I could have one.

I told him everything that I had said in the meetings before, how I did not like masks or Halloween—in fact, I stated that it was a phobia. I went on to say how uncomfortable this phobia made me feel. Then he asked something that had never been brought up in any other meeting: "Have you ever watched the film *Halloween*?"

Just the thought of it made me start to shake, but I managed to answer. "No—I wouldn't want to either. I couldn't even watch the advert."

As the meeting progressed, he also asked if I was afraid of any other masks—for example, headscarves or surgical masks. I pointed out that these were not scary, so I was fine with them. He was going through everything with a fine-tooth comb, not missing anything and covering everything. He asked if I liked pumpkins, and I told him that I didn't mind them and I wasn't frightened of them.

The subject of Mardi Gras and Christmas masks was brought up. Again, I told Derek that horror masks were the cause of my phobia—something like Mardi Gras was colourful and bright, so I wasn't frightened of them. The same for Christmas, as—to me—they were classed as 'happy masks'.

Derek went on to justify why they were using masks to raise money. He sat there and told me that this was a bit of creative fun for people to get involved in while raising money for charity.

I took a deep breath and replied, "I appreciate that it's for a charity, but I have a phobia, and that will never change."

At one point in the meeting, I got upset because he asked about people and children dressing up around Halloween. I tried to explain without getting tearful about a time when I tried to go trick-or-treating with my friend and her children, but I found myself keeping my distance because I just could not cope with everyone being dressed up. I even tried to emphasise that when I came home after that event, I saw a wolf knocking my door and panicked. Even though I knew it was someone dressed up, that didn't make a difference to me. I hid in my car until they disappeared, and then ran inside. This had all happened a few years ago when I hadn't known I had a phobia—I'd honestly just thought I did not like the season.

Derek seemed to be listening, but to be honest, I thought it went in one ear and out the other. By the time the meeting was over, I was a nervous wreck.

CHAPTER 67

After the meeting, I sat down, feeling numb. Michael got me a drink from the machine and sat with me.

"You did really well in there," he said.

I looked at him as I took a sip of my drink. "It doesn't feel like it. It feels like going around in circles, except this time, I felt as if I was being poked and prodded until I was at breaking point."

Michael laughed slightly. "I get what you are saying—it did feel like that at times. Having those couple of breaks during the meeting meant you were able to get your thoughts together before continuing, and I think you did really well."

I finished my drink. "I just feel very drained. I feel like I've been put through hell. They're questioning everything I do and, to be honest, it feels like I'm the one on trial and no one else. What do you think will happen?"

He was about to answer, but someone interrupted our conversation to get his advice. Michael was always in demand as a union rep, which was no surprise because he was really good.

I got myself another drink and, when I got back, Michael answered my question. "Derek is a good manager; he will interview the others, but he's often hard to read when it comes to what outcome he'll give."

"Then I guess we'll have to wait and see."

* * *

When I arrived home, the house was empty. I tried calling Mason, but it kept going to answerphone. There was no point leaving a message—he never retrieved them.

I spent the afternoon watching TV and eating anything and everything. Then I heard a familiar voice—my brother, returning from work.

He walked into the living room. When he saw me, he said, "Have you been sent home again?"

I shot him a nasty look. "No, I have not been sent home…again. I finished work after my meeting and came home."

"Well, I'm not staying, because I have a hot date. Once I've changed, I'll be out of your hair again." And with that, he disappeared.

I'd started watching TV again when I heard a voice say, "Finally, you are going to crack, and then I will win."

I froze, panic setting in as I heard the voice. Clenching my eyes shut, I screamed in anger, trying to block it out. All I heard in return was a laugh.

"The stronger the fear, the more powerful I become, and you feed me so well. Autumn is just around the corner, so we will be seeing each other very soon. But until then, bye.'

Whatever it was, this voice gave me the creeps. It loved to taunt and frighten me, and the problem was it worked.

I was on the edge. Between my phobia and work, I was becoming more stressed out. When I'd first freaked out and told work, all I wanted them to do was to acknowledge I had this unusual phobia and to agree that no masks or decorations would be put up in the office until an agreed time, which I would take as a holiday, and then take them down before I was due back in work. It was a reasonable request, but all I'd had from work was a stonewall approach to this. They couldn't even follow their own next steps. Because of them, I was left feeling upset, hurt and terrified to go back into work as I no longer felt safe.

It was no wonder I was still hearing the voice and thinking more and more about Halloween. The nightmares still plagued me. I could only hope that soon work would get the message, I could get on with my life and find a way of dealing with this phobia, and hope that the stress would die down.

CHAPTER 68

Mason walked in the door in the early hours of the morning, and that was when things kicked off.

"Have you calmed down, Em?"

I looked at him, puzzled. "I am calm. What are you on about?"

He hadn't even started getting undressed when he replied, "Well, when I mentioned that I was having to go away tomorrow night, you were being unreasonable."

"Mase, that was hours ago. Why are you holding onto this? All I was trying to emphasise was that I didn't want you away for the night... You know I wanted you here with me—I thought I was being romantic."

"You thought that was being romantic, basically telling me not to go away? I have to go away occasionally with this job—thankfully not a lot, but when I need to, I have to. I don't need you having a go at me."

I racked my brains as to why he was being so off with me. Yes, I'd said I didn't want him to go away, but that hadn't been unreasonable. "I wasn't having a go at you. I just wanted you to stay here—and in some sort of way, I'd hope you would be the same with me."

"Well, we're not talking about you—this is about me and my job. I'm not in the mood to talk about this anymore. I need sleep."

He quickly undressed, got under the covers and turned his back on me without a kiss goodnight. When I tried to cuddle up to him, he shook me off and moved closer to the edge of the bed. Suddenly, I was left there, wondering what had just happened and why he was acting like this. Then the tears came, and I cried myself to sleep.

* * *

In the morning, Mason walked in the kitchen and grabbed himself a cup of tea. He looked at me blankly and was about to walk out the kitchen when he stopped dead in his tracks and turned to face me.

"I'm sorry about last night. I shouldn't have taken it out on you. I should have had a discussion and not a go. It was just yesterday was a really stressful day, and now I've got to stay overnight for a meeting that I could really do with not attending, because at the moment the store is falling apart, and I need to be there."

I gave him half a smile. "If you had told me, then that would have been better than just having a go at me. Is there anything else I need to know?"

"When I get back from this meeting, I will be doing a lot more hours at the store—basically a twelve-hour shift per day—"

"What?!"

"The duty manager has phoned in sick and I have a few more staff off as well and deliveries haven't been turning up…sorry, I'll correct that—they have been turning up, but things have been missing, and therefore we're not getting the things we need for the store. I've also had back-to-back meetings the last couple of days within the store, so now I have to step up the hours to cover everybody else."

"So this means I won't be seeing you a lot this week."

"No." He looked at his watch. "I have to go to work and then I have to drive straight to the hotel for this meeting tomorrow. I should be back about ten o'clock tomorrow evening."

He quickly kissed me and then disappeared out the front door. I followed him, as something was wrong. He was about to pull away when he noticed me approaching the car.

He opened the window and said flatly, "What's wrong?"

I didn't hold back. "I could ask you the same thing. So, Mason, what is wrong?"

He put his head on the steering wheel and muttered something.

"Mason, what did you say?"

"I was pulled into a meeting and told not to disappear from work." Shock hit me as he continued. "Remember when I picked you up from work due to your phobia a while back? Well, I was told off."

"Oh, Mason, I'm sorry…I…"

"It's OK—it was just the once. The other times were either before or after work or on my day off."

I glanced away, feeling guilty, but he smiled. "I'll ring tonight when I get to the hotel. Love you."

"You too."

Then he drove away.

CHAPTER 69

When I got to work, someone new was sitting at Leo's desk. It was Kim, the team leader who had taken notes during the meeting with Helen. She came over, introduced herself as if we'd never met and asked if we could have a catch-up. We went in one of the side rooms and had a talk.

"Where is Leo?" I asked.

"He got a promotion."

"He didn't tell the team!"

She smiled at me. "Apparently he applied a few weeks ago and was notified on the weekend, so we had to move quickly. That's probably why he hasn't been in. Anyway, I know that the grievance is still pending against myself and others, but I hope we can work together as part of the team."

"I would like that. I hope you can understand this is not personal; it's just I want things to be cleared up."

"I do understand, and I appreciate your honesty. So, I will be the new team leader for the team. If you do have any problems, please feel free to come to me and we will go over them."

We spoke for a bit longer and then made our way back to our desks. Michael was waiting for me when I got back. We went to the breakout area to talk and he told me that the interviews with everyone concerned had been conducted and a decision had been reached. Derek wanted another meeting after lunch, if that was OK. I said that that was fine and Michael gave me the time. We agreed to meet after lunch to go through anything before the meeting.

* * *

Later that afternoon I was back in the meeting room with Derek and Grace as the notetaker. We exchanged pleasantries and then the meeting began.

Derek leaned back in the chair slightly. "As you are now aware, I have come to a decision about the grievance you put in against these people." He reeled off their names, and said, "I do have to ask, as it's been brought to my attention—you were offered a position in-store while we carried out the charity event. The reason I have brought this up is I wanted to know why you did not take up the offer?"

I took a deep breath before replying. "My job is here, in an office. I have never worked in-store before and I felt that the company could have been more accommodating rather than sending me somewhere else to avoid dealing with the situation."

He nodded that he understood and then asked a few more questions before finally telling me his decision.

"I interviewed everyone concerned, and a few of them were puzzled as to why they were being investigated when they did not know about your phobia."

I sat there, totally bewildered by what was coming out of his mouth. Each person I had named on the grievance knew about my phobia because they had all been present at the meetings, except Carol, who'd been unfortunate enough to see me first-hand when the very first incident had taken place.

"They all knew about my phobia," I firmly replied. "About the masks, and Halloween, so they cannot say they were not aware."

Michael shook his head in disbelief.

Derek continued, "I feel that, on this occasion, none of the people mentioned in your grievance are to blame for what happened. I understand this is a difficult time for you, especially around Halloween when your phobia becomes more prominent, but as I've stated, I don't think all these people can be held accountable for something that's not their fault."

After that, we quickly wrapped up the meeting.

Outside, I was furious. Michael tried his best to calm me down, but I said firmly, "I cannot believe what he just said in there. They all knew about this phobia because I had explained it enough, through every meeting."

"Well, I would suggest that you take this to a second-stage grievance, which will mean it will be heard by the call centre manager," Michael stated.

I looked at him with surprise. "So I can take this further? I don't have to accept his decision?"

"No, you do not have to accept his decision and, to be honest, I would take it further. As you stated in the meeting, they did know about this phobia."

I suddenly perked up, feeling that there was a real hope here. "Yes, I want to appeal this, and as quickly as possible."

Michael smiled. "Then I will let them know that you want to appeal this, and they will be in contact with you."

CHAPTER 70

A week later, I walked in from work and went to the kitchen. A pile of mail was on the side. As I went through it, I found a letter from my work. It read:

Following receipt of your second-stage grievance, I am writing to invite you to a meeting.

The meeting is with Tim, the centre manager, and the head of personnel manager, Jane. It will take place at the call centre on 16th September at 10 AM.

I digested the letter. At least they weren't prolonging this. I just hoped Michael would be free to be there for the meeting, otherwise it would have to be rescheduled.

* * *

When I arrived at work, I logged in, put myself straight into code because I couldn't see any team leaders around, and went to find Michael. He was taking calls, which was unusual because he was normally busy with union-related issues instead. I pulled up a chair and sat beside him, waiting for him to finish his call.

When he finished, he put himself in code and turned his attention to me. "Let me guess: you need me for another meeting?"

I laughed at his directness. "I got the letter about the second-stage grievance this morning and they want to do it on the sixteenth, starting at ten o'clock. Will you be available for that day?"

He checked his calendar on the computer. "I do have a meeting that day, but it's one I can reschedule. I've been with you in all these meetings since the beginning, so it's only fair for me to see this to the end."

I watched him take off his glasses and clean them. "I appreciate that; I just don't think they're going to listen."

Michael put his glasses back on and said, "The problem here is that they're following a strict process instead of thinking about this logically. This could be rectified very simply if they didn't follow the process to the letter. The first time this occurred, then yes, I could understand them saying they had no idea, but now so many people know, they can't use that as an excuse anymore."

I noticed how quiet it was around the area where Michael sat. "How come it's so quiet around here?" I asked.

"They've done a bit of reshuffling, so I think it means this area has more of the night shift. It's great for us because it's easier to take calls—you can actually hear them."

"I better get back to taking calls before they send out a search party to look for me!"

He laughed. "They can be a bit like that sometimes! But I'll see you on the sixteenth, the day of the meeting."

* * *

While I was on lunch, I remembered to check my phone. It had been a few hours since I'd last looked, which was unusual because normally I couldn't wait to check my phone. I had received a text from Mason: *Have you got a day off tomorrow? If you have the day off maybe we can do something.*

Just my luck—my fiancé had the day off and I was in work.

I quickly replied: *Don't have day off, but will see what I can do.*

When I got back to my desk, I checked to see if I could book the day off, but unfortunately it wasn't possible.

I sent another text: *I tried but cannot get day off, but when I finish maybe we can do something then?* After I sent the message, the hours dragged by through the rest of my shift.

* * *

I was really hungry when I got home, so I made myself some food and ate alone in the kitchen. However, I didn't enjoy the food—it was just something to relieve my hunger.

My phone went and when I answered it, it was Mason.

"Hi, Em—how was work?"

I put the kettle on again. "Work was work, but I did receive a letter from them stating that they're going to hear the grievance for a second time. This time, it will be heard by the centre manager."

"Hopefully they'll listen to you this time and it will all get sorted. I wanted to let you know the meeting I'm in has gone on longer than expected, so don't wait for me if you need food."

"Thanks for letting me know, but I've already eaten—I was starving."

"What time do you finish work tomorrow?"

"Hopefully at four o'clock. Why? What do you have planned?"

Mason laughed slightly. "I was thinking about

just something simple—cooking food and maybe a movie?"

I smiled at the thought of quality time. "That sounds nice. Could you pick me up from work then?"

I could tell Mason was happy when he replied, "That won't be a problem. I have to get back to work, so will speak to you later."

We said our goodbyes and then hung up.

CHAPTER 71

When Mason picked me up from work, he had a letter in his hand.

"I thought this might be important," he said as he gave me a kiss, "so that's why I brought it with me rather than wait."

I opened the letter.

You have been referred to us by your doctor. This letter confirms that you are now on the waiting list to be seen and we will write to you in due course.

This was the letter from the hospital that I'd been waiting for, to see the psychiatrist.

"Was the letter important?" Mason asked.

"It's a letter from the hospital; it looks like they're willing to see me, but there's a wait."

"This is good news. Hopefully now, this won't be a long wait and you'll be seen sooner rather than later."

I sighed. "I just hope they can help me so that my nightmare can be over."

"Don't bank on it," the voice said. I didn't react, but part of me believed it.

* * *

I'd started cooking dinner and I could hear Mason in the living room. It sounded as if he was in the middle of the war zone, he was making so much noise.

"What are you doing in there?" I called.

"I'm just looking for something," he shouted back.

As I got to the living room to see what all the fuss was about, he shouted, "I found it."

I shook my head and asked, "What was it you were looking for?"

"I heard this band on the radio and liked their music, so I bought the album and wanted to play it."

"Then play it, and then come in the kitchen and help me."

Mason put on the music and came out to the kitchen. It was nice just to be a couple again—it felt like we hadn't been like that for a long time because of work and this phobia.

Mason told me about the meeting he'd had to attend and broke the news to me that the meeting hadn't concluded, so he had to go away next month to finalise the meeting.

As the music continued in the background, I said, "Never heard this before, but I like this music. What are they called?"

"Lady Antebellum," Mason said, stirring one of the pots.

I started singing along—I shouldn't have because I didn't have a singing voice, but when I heard one song, I related to it. I checked the song's name on the back of the CD case—"One Day You Will". It spoke to me. Most people interpret songs differently but, to me, this song explained how I felt when I was faced with my phobia and the problems that I had encountered because of it. It summed up my life with this phobia. I felt pain because I could see no way out, but one day, there would be a release from this and I would come out the other side.

I just hoped that was true.

The phobia was bad enough, but with work adding to it, some days I felt I would never get over this and I would be forever in this vicious circle.

Mason brought me out of my thoughts. "Em, I've been calling you. Food is ready."

We sat down and started eating. "Are these meetings away going to become a regular thing?"

Mason looked at me. "I hope not, because before I took the job, I was told once, maybe twice a year. When is the next meeting for you?"

"Next week on the sixteenth, but I don't know how much more I can take. When the masks were first displayed, and then they offered me alternative work, and then the meeting, and now a second meeting..."

"Em, slow down."

"I'm getting stressed and they don't even care."

Mason held my hand. "Well, I care," he said sweetly.

"Thank you," I said, smiling back. "You must be the only one."

CHAPTER 72

The charity event had taken place during the summer and with all the arguments and meetings, it was soon September. Yet I still had another meeting to go. I was very nervous about meeting the centre manager. I had heard many stories about him, and they were all good, but that didn't change the fact that he intimidated me. Tim was tall, a big man, and he had a very strong accent, probably from the London area. If there was a work party, he would be there, with the ones on the front line, as we called it. Everyone said he was very approachable and he was friendly but, for some reason, I felt that I couldn't approach him. He was the manager, the boss. However, I was going to have to face my fear. I was about to sit in front of him for my grievance, and I was terrified.

Michael looked at me with concern. "Are you alright?"

I was starting to shake. "Honestly, I'm terrified. I've never been in the room with Tim—am I supposed to call him sir?"

Michael chuckled. "Tim looks intimidating, but I can say from experience that he's not. He's down to earth and very aware of what goes on around here."

I was shocked. "So are you saying that he could have known about my phobia before the meeting?"

"It's likely he was made aware, but he puts

trust in the managers to deal with issues. Tim is always in meetings, very rarely in his office at the centre, but as I said, it doesn't mean he doesn't know what goes on. His secretary probably gives him most of the gossip."

My head was spinning. "I feel sick."

He looked at me sympathetically. "All you have to do is be honest with him and you will be fine. You really don't have anything to worry about—he's not this monster, just so you know."

A slender woman approached us. "Sorry about the delay in the meeting," she said, "but we are ready to start, if you are?"

Michael glanced at me and then back to the woman. "We'll just get a drink and then we'll be right with you."

She smiled and left us to it.

Michael glanced over at me and said with concern, "Remember what I said—he's not scary, and all you have to do is be honest with him."

As I tried to breathe, my nerves were getting the better of me. "OK," I replied.

We got our drinks and made our way to the meeting room. I put my bag down and suddenly, because I was so nervous, I had to excuse myself to use the bathroom. In the cubicle, I took slow breaths to calm myself down. I'd never wanted the grievance to get this far, but now it was here, I was not going to back down. At the end of the day, things had to change.

I kept telling myself, over and over, *He is a normal person, he is not scary and all you have to do is tell the truth.*

I walked back into the room and sat down.

"Are you ready?" Michael asked.

"I think so." Then I turned to face Tim. "Sorry about that."

He smiled at me and said, "We all need to use the bathroom, so there's no need to apologise."

He looked at the lady who would be taking the notes, and then back at Michael and me. "Now, before we start the meeting, I just want you to know that anything you say is in confidence and, if you need a break, then please let me know. Also, knowing the nature of this meeting, there was a picture on the wall of myself in a mask, but I have removed it so you aren't frightened. This is so you are comfortable when explaining what has been going on."

I was already nervously playing with my hands, but I tried my best to make eye contact with him. "Thank you—that was very thoughtful of you."

"As you know, my name is Tim, and this is head of personnel in head office, Jane." He gestured to the woman taking notes.

She smiled at me. "As Tim said, you do not have to be nervous about saying anything in here, and if you need a break, then you can take one at any time."

CHAPTER 73

It was one of the toughest meetings I had ever encountered.

Tim was warm and friendly towards me. He and Jane came across as very sympathetic throughout the meeting, but that didn't stop my nerves. The meeting started like most of the others, with him asking questions and me explaining about my phobia. I answered his questions as best as I could.

"Tell me, Emily—if you see an image of a mask on television, does this affect you?"

I was still rubbing my hands when I answered him. "When I see the image live on a screen, yes, it does affect me."

"I have read through the previous meetings and have a little understanding of how this may impact you, but could you explain to me in detail—how does this affect you?"

I felt like I was going around in circles, not because he'd asked the question, but because I was repeating myself in meeting after meeting.

As I was explaining how this impacted me, I burst into tears. I got a tissue from my handbag, but Tim quickly stopped what he was in the middle of saying and said to me, "I think it's time for us to take a break. Would twenty minutes be OK?"

As I was cleaning up my tears, I nodded in agreement and quickly left his office.

Michael followed me to the breakout area and made me sit down while he got me a drink.

"I can see that you're struggling," he said, "but you are doing well."

I tried to compose myself and replied, "I don't know what's wrong with me—I'm so nervous in there."

"I think it's because it's been meeting after meeting and you're having to explain yourself over and over again. From what I know about you and this phobia, this is not a good time of year anyway."

"Now all the kids are back at school, the stores are already putting up the decorations for Halloween, and this means I'm stuck at home again."

"Have you heard from the psychiatrist yet?"

"I did have a letter from them; it basically said I was on the waiting list, so now it's just a waiting game as to when."

"Well, hopefully seeing the psychiatrist can help you, and then you can have normality."

I did like how to-the-point Michael was.

"Normality for me..." I said. "I don't even remember what that was. Before they put the decorations in here and plunged me into my worst hell ever, I was never aware of how I really felt, and now it's like my world is crashing down around me."

"It can seem like that, but from what you have told me in our previous conversations, you have a loving boyfriend—sorry, fiancé—at home who has been there for you all the way."

"Mason is a sweetie, and if it wasn't for him I think I would've fallen apart a long time ago. I just want them to acknowledge what they have done, find a middle ground and then move on."

"I understand what you're saying. How are you feeling now?"

I was still a nervous wreck, but I had cleared up my tears. Thanks to Michael and his normal conversation, I did feel better.

Knowing that in a few minutes we'd be back in that meeting room, I excused myself to use the bathroom because I didn't want to have to leave again so abruptly. I looked in the mirror and was tidying myself up when I heard, "You know this is never going to end, right? And as the weeks go on, I will be in your thoughts more than ever before.'

I wanted to scream, to shout at the voice, and it took all my energy to stop myself and hold back.

"Go on, ignore me. But I'm still going to be here."

"You may still be here," I said under my breath so no one else could hear, "but if I have anything to do with it, not for long."

"That's what you think." And then there was silence.

CHAPTER 74

As the meeting continued, the more the stress and nerves got to me. Since the summer charity event, it had dawned on me that masks and horror could rear their ugly heads at any time of year, not just October. I'd always thought my phobia would be seasonal, but it wasn't. It could affect me at any time of the year. The fact that work was responsible, especially in this case, had made me a nervous wreck. These stress levels were like nothing I'd experienced before. I hated being in the building—when I was there, I was very aware of my surroundings and constantly looking over my shoulder. I'd often considered leaving, but unfortunately, it was good money. I'd say I hated it, but I never minded the job itself, or the people. It was just the fact that they wouldn't acknowledge the part they had played, and that they were compounding my stress.

As I answered the questions thrown at me, I was very quiet and subdued. I found it hard to make eye contact with Tim and always found myself fiddling with my hands as I tried to keep my head above water and answer with truth and honesty. There were a few occasions that Jane interjected with questions of her own, which I thought was not allowed by the notetaker. However, since she was the head personnel manager, it did make sense that she wanted a full picture.

I felt as if I were on trial. They didn't shout at

me or openly accuse me, but when I answered the questions they directed at me, they either gave their opinions or asked another question. They were bombarding me with so many things that I was retreating into myself. All I wanted to do was hide.

It also didn't help that it was now September and Halloween was only weeks away. Since I'd started to get answers from the doctor, I'd noticed my personality changed the closer the dreaded month got.

I needed so many breaks during this meeting and I felt terrible because of it. Everyone in the centre was judging me, watching me. They must have thought I was pathetic and stupid. Maybe they were right.

I couldn't help but think like that—I was in an awful state. During this meeting, it took everything I had to just stay there and deal with their bombardment of questions. Due to my stress levels, I lost count of how many times I wanted to walk out of that meeting and run away.

However, I stayed and endured those few hours and I was so relieved to hear the words, "If you do not have anything else to say, then I would like to take this opportunity to thank you for attending the meeting, as I know it's been difficult for you. I would now like to adjourn to make a decision, so we will call you back in an hour."

Shaking, I nodded and replied quietly, "Thank you for listening. I don't have anything to add to the meeting, so I will see you in an hour."

When I came out of that room, it was like I could breathe again. Michael took me away from the area and we headed to the canteen. He sat me down and asked calmly, "How are you feeling?"

"I could be doing better. I can't believe I almost

crumbled in there, but I was so nervous and it just got to me."

"I did notice, but I have to say you did really well. I suggest you get something to eat, and then we'll hear what Tim has to say in an hour. Unfortunately, I have to go and see someone else because they have an issue, so I'll be lucky if I get a sandwich before we go back."

I smiled as best I could. "Thank you. How did you think it went?"

"He went into a lot of detail, wanting to know in more depth about the phobia and how it affected you. So, I'm not sure."

"OK. See you in an hour."

CHAPTER 75

The hour passed so slowly as I waited for a conclusion to this meeting. When I got back to my desk, Kim approached me.

"How did the meeting go?" she asked.

I was surprised at her interest, considering she was one of the reasons why the grievance was taking place, but her concern seemed genuine.

"I was a nervous wreck in there, and to be honest, I just want it over and done with."

She gave me half a smile. "You will be fine; I know it."

Even though I'd taken out a grievance against her, we hadn't let it affect our working relationship. We did genuinely get on, despite everything surrounding the phobia. It was nice that she harboured no ill will towards me.

"Thanks," I said.

"Also, Michael has been looking for you, because they want to start the meeting now."

"It hasn't been an hour yet!"

"Well, Michael said he would meet you in the breakout area near the meeting room."

I quickly re-entered the code on the computer and made my way to the breakout room. Michael was talking to someone and I waited patiently while he finished the conversation. Once the person had walked away, I said, "They did say an hour?"

"I know they did. However, it's not unheard of for them to come back with the decision sooner, especially at this level."

"Is this a bad sign though?"

"We will have to see, but there's no point jumping the gun just yet."

My hands started to shake again, and suddenly, I was overcome with nerves, as I was earlier in the meeting. "I'm starting to feel nervous again," I told Michael.

He looked at me and said, "Just stay calm. Listen to what he has to say before you respond."

I nodded in agreement as we waited outside.

We were called back into the room and that's when things got serious. Tim still had a big smile on his face, as he had throughout the meeting— as that was just him, a friendly person who got on with everyone.

"Are you OK to continue?"

"Yes."

"As you know, we took an hour adjournment, so I could check through all the paperwork and make my decision. Well, I have come to a decision.

"I understand that what you have experienced, and what you are going through, is a terrible thing. You state that because these people knew about the phobia, they did not advise you about this charity event and the use of masks. Having looked over all the meetings and evidence, I have concluded that these people were not to blame for what has happened.

"However, I do acknowledge that, as a centre, we could do more to help. I will email all management so that they are aware of your condition. This will mean that, in future, we will let you know of future events if they are related to your phobia. We will allow you time off during these periods, so that you can manage it the best way you know how, although we cannot give you extra days off for this. You will have to take it out of holidays or unpaid.

"Having said all this, I cannot control what is on the TVs around the centre—for example, in the breakout area—because as you are aware, this is for everyone. So, what comes on during the adverts has nothing to do with us.

"How do you feel about what I've said?"

I took a moment before I went to answer. "I understand what you have said, but I do disagree with part of your decision. Management knew of my condition, and therefore should have informed me, as I was not in work to have prior knowledge beforehand. I do, however, thank you for acknowledging that I would need time off during this difficult period. However, I feel that I should have a few extra days for this period, as this means I cannot take any summer holidays off because I have to save it for this time. When it comes to the TVs, I appreciate what you say—they are in the breakout areas and cannot be controlled by yourself."

I didn't ask for the extra days of holiday because I wanted to go away, but because I was fed up of losing money because of my phobia. None of us had many holidays, anyway. I didn't want to use mine up covering for my phobia, only to miss out on the rest of the year.

"As I said, you won't be allowed extra holidays, as that would not be fair on everybody else. The people that you named in the grievance are not to blame, as some stated they didn't know you had a phobia."

Did he just make a slip of the tongue? He'd stated earlier that they were not to blame, but now I was hearing that some of them had said they didn't know I had a phobia? Well, that was a lie. They all knew.

I couldn't believe it. I'd sat here, an absolute wreck, throughout the last few hours of the meeting, and now he was telling me that some of them didn't know. How dare they!

"Can I ask what you mean by 'they didn't know'?"

He looked taken aback by my question. "I will not name the person or persons that stated they were not aware."

"Not aware! If you read the meetings, which you said you did, then you would know the words mask and Halloween were mentioned several times. So, whether they were taking the meeting or were a notetaker, they would have knowledge of the phobia and how it affected me."

He did not lose his composure once throughout my statement. "As I stated," he replied calmly, "they were unaware of your phobia. I have made my decision, and that means no one will be held accountable, but we will allow you time off during the period. If no time is available, we will make sure you have the time off."

I was seething inside, but there was nothing I could do to make him change his mind. So I took a deep breath, smiled, and replied calmly as I could. "OK."

There was a lot more I wanted to say, but from past experience, I knew how the meeting would go. There was no point kicking off, as much as I wanted to.

After the papers were signed, I quickly left the room and went to get a drink.

Michael found me and said, "I have to admit, you do have a point—they all knew."

"Then why will he not admit that?"

"He likes to think of his managers as being able to cope with everyday situations. If he were to acknowledge that they'd made a mistake, then that wouldn't look good."

My eyes wanted to pop out of my head, but it wasn't Michael I was mad at.

"That is the reason he removes blame from them? This is ridiculous. You were there in every meeting; each manager and team leader knew about my phobia. They are even the ones that recommended I get help—next steps, they called it. Yet here we are, and I'm the one following the next steps that they have given me, and yet they are not following the same steps that they gave themselves." Now I was on a rant. "They told me to not only get help, but that they would either phone me, or I should phone into work to see if any decorations were up. This way, they could do the walk-around before I entered the building so I'd know I was safe. But here we are, and no one is to blame… Oh wait, except me."

Michael didn't look surprised at my little outburst. To be fair to the man, he was a very good listener, which was why everyone came to him for union help.

"You have every right to be angry, and I don't blame you. I know it's your home time now, so I would suggest going home, gathering your thoughts, and we will speak about this tomorrow."

I nodded in agreement. "I think I need time to calm down as well. See you tomorrow."

CHAPTER 76

Sitting at home, I was deep in thought. All the meetings over the last couple of years had been pointless. The company didn't care but expected me to bend over backwards.

Suddenly, I heard a voice from behind me. "Sis, are you OK?"

I looked around and saw my brother walk towards me and sit down.

"I could be better," I replied. "The meeting didn't go as well as I'd hoped. I'd even go as far as to say it went badly."

Mark looked shocked. "This isn't good. What happened?"

I told him of the events that had taken place in the meeting. How no one was made accountable for what had happened.

He shook his head in disbelief. "This absolutely sucks. All you want them to do is to acknowledge that they could have been a bit more understanding."

"Yes, you would think, but they can't or won't. I'm not sure which."

Mark gave me a big hug. "What you need is a large drink."

I smiled and replied, "I think you may be right."

There was nothing in the fridge, so Mark decided to take me out. I texted Mason, letting him know where I would be, and then left the house with Mark.

At the pub, he bought me a drink.

"Drink up," he said, giving it to me.

I shouldn't have, but I was really stressed out after the meeting, so I knocked the drink back. Mark smiled at me and knocked his back as well. "Another?" he asked.

He didn't wait for an answer before going to the bar again. Soon enough, he was back with more drinks.

"I'm starving. Fancy anything to eat?" he said as he grabbed the menu.

"Maybe. I could do with something to eat, but I don't know what I fancy."

"If you're worried about the money, don't be— this is on me."

I looked at him in shock. "You're finally treating me?" I said sarcastically.

He shot back a look as he finished his drink. "Don't look so surprised. I am capable of treating my sister!"

I had just finished my drink when I replied, "Well, I *am* surprised, because when you moved in with me ages ago, you didn't have any money, and now you have a job and are finally treating me, it's just weird."

"Yes, it's strange, but at least it's happening. Now, being the good brother that I am... When are you getting married?"

I almost choked on my drink. "In case you've forgotten, I've only just got engaged. It doesn't help that I haven't seen enough of Mason to be able to set any dates, let alone plan a wedding."

I could see that he was trying to distract me from the day's events, and I was very grateful. So, to change the subject, I asked him about his life. More importantly, his love life.

"How long you been seeing this girl?"

Mark's eyes narrowed as he looked at me. "Do

you want me to buy you more drinks?"

I smiled at him. "Relax, Mark—this isn't an interrogation. I was just asking a question. I mean, you haven't even told me her name."

"Fine, her name is Anne, and I've been seeing her for about a month. The reason I haven't brought her to the house is because the last time I brought someone back, that ended in disaster."

"So, what does she look like?"

He rolled his eyes at me and answered, "I can do better than that—I can show you," as he brought up the pictures on his mobile.

"You aren't going to show me any naked pictures, are you?"

He pulled his phone back towards himself. "Do you want to see a picture of her or not?" he said firmly.

I pulled the glass away from my mouth before I took a sip. "Sorry. Show me a picture."

When I saw the picture, I had to admit, it was the first time in a while Mark had looked happy. She was a brunette with shoulder-length hair— this did surprise me, because he normally went for blondes. She had a nice smile and green eyes. I didn't know if she was the one, but I had a sense they would be together for a while.

CHAPTER 77

Mark and I were in the middle of eating when Mason turned up. He kissed me and proceeded to eat some of my food.

I tapped his hand. "Get your own."

He smiled at me and took a chip from my plate as he got up to go to the bar. I shot him a look.

"Do you want another drink?" he asked.

Truth was, I did, but I had work in the morning. "Just a Coke, please."

As I was eating my food, I noticed many people going into the beer garden to have a cigarette. Problem was, I was in the middle of giving up, but at that point, with all the stress that had been going on, I really needed one. It took all of my willpower to stop myself from going outside with everybody else.

"Do you miss it?" Mark asked.

"Yes, all the time. Right now, I could really do with one."

"Well, I think you're doing really well by not going out there."

When I looked down at my plate, there was no more food left. "Since you're buying me drinks and food," I said to Mark, "does that include dessert?"

"I think you might have bled me dry," he said as he laughed. "Go on, you can have dessert."

Mason came back from the bar and put the drinks down. "My food's going to be thirty minutes."

Suddenly, Mark and Mason were talking about

football and boy stuff. To me, it was boring.

"Mark, do you want any dessert?" I interrupted them. "Because, if so, pick one and I'll go to the bar for us."

After about five minutes, he finally picked a dessert and gave me the money. I gladly went to the bar to escape their conversation. When I got back to the table, Mark was in the middle of telling Mason about his new girlfriend and the stuff they got up to.

"Could you keep things like that to yourself, Mark?" I interjected.

Mark had a big grin on his face. "You only don't like what I say because it's the truth," he replied cheekily.

"Shut up," I snapped back, but he continued giving Mason all the dirty details in front of me.

Finally, the desserts turned up, stopping Mark in his tracks. He stayed quiet while he ate.

Mason was getting impatient. "Where is my food?" he asked.

"Mase, if you're worried, then go and ask at the bar."

"I'm starving."

This conversation went on for a few minutes until Mason went to the bar. When he came back, he said, "They said it'll be five minutes. Anyway, Em—I forgot to ask—how did the meeting go?"

"As you would expect, terrible. No one is to blame, but I can have time off over Halloween. That was pretty much it... Almost forgot, I cried in the meeting as I was a bag of nerves."

Mark interrupted the conversation. "Mason, when are you going to get married?"

I rolled my eyes and glared at my brother as Mason answered.

"We've just got engaged, but we'll discuss it

soon. Now, if we're talking about stuff… When are you moving out?"

I grinned as brother fidgeted.

"I'm not in any rush—are you? Besides, what would you do without me around?"

"Have the place to ourselves!" Mason exclaimed.

Mark, being Mark, replied casually, "You need the rent money and…"

"Rent money? What rent money?"

Mark said flatly, "I'm paying for tonight, aren't I?" as if that would get him out of the hole he had dug.

Mason called him on it. "In that case, you owe me money for my drinks and food, mate."

"Fine," Mark said as he slammed thirty pounds on the table. "Will that cover your side?"

Mason picked up the money. "Yes," he said sarcastically. "Yes, it will…mate."

Sometimes I wondered if they really were grown men, but I had to admit, it was nice to have a break from all the stress. I loved them both for that.

CHAPTER 78

When I returned to work the following day, things went on as if nothing had happened. An hour into my shift, Michael turned up to speak to me. He stood there patiently as he waited for me to finish my call.

"I've just been given this by HR," he said, handing me a form. "They want you to sign it to say that you agree with the outcome of the grievance."

I was mortified—they wanted me to say that I agreed with everything in that meeting.

"They're kidding, right?"

"Unfortunately not. They want you to sign it but, as your union rep, I can say to you that you don't have to sign it, if you don't wish to."

"Well, I'm not going to sign it, because I don't agree with everything that was said in the meeting. Especially the part about not holding anyone accountable. As we both know, the people on that grievance knew about this phobia."

"I agree. So, do you want me to tell them that you are not signing it?"

I looked Michael straight in the eye. "Tell them from me: I am not signing this."

While we were talking, a woman from HR came over to my desk. "Do you have that document signed?" she asked.

This woman had a nerve to even ask that question.

"I have talked to Emily about this," Michael

stated to her, "and she has said—and I agree with her—that she is not signing this document as we don't agree with everything that was said in the meeting."

"You have to sign the document," the woman insisted.

"I don't have to sign any document that I do not wish to. And just so you know, I am not signing it."

She did not look pleased at all. "Then I'm going to have to seek advice on this, because I'm pretty sure you'll have to sign this document whether you agree with it or not."

When she had left my desk, Michael turned to me. "If you can meet me in the breakout area, we will discuss this further."

I went over to Kim's desk. "They want me to sign a document and I am refusing to do so," I said to her. "Michael wants to discuss this further with me—is it okay to see him in the breakout area?"

"Absolutely—just put yourself in code before you go. Is it anything I can help you with?"

"I appreciate the gesture, but I think Michael has everything in hand."

I went to the breakout area with Michael and we discussed the previous day, and the meeting.

"After the meeting concluded and their decision was given," he said, "I spoke to the union chairman. I was advised to speak to the union directly. They feel that your case isn't being heard properly, so they are looking into taking things further."

"Does this mean taking it to court?" I enquired.

"It may be possible to take it to court, but that's why the union is looking into it further—to see what can be done."

After the first meeting, I'd been so angry that I

wanted to seek legal action, but I'd been advised against it at that early stage and asked to follow the process of the grievance. Now that it might be a possibility, I was taken aback.

"Well, let's see what the union can come up with and I guess we'll take it from there. They do know it's about a phobia, right?" I asked.

"They are aware of your phobia, but it has been mentioned that this might come under a mental disability. That's what they're trying to find out. It would also help your case if you were seeing the psychiatrist, but you're still on the waiting list. I've also advised them of this."

"Thank you. I didn't think that this could go any further… It might not, but at least there's a bit of hope, I guess."

"They could have held the people that knew about the phobia to account, but they've chosen to ignore everything that has been in the meetings," Michael stated. "I appreciate that some of them have been better than others about the phobia, but we'll just have to wait to hear from the union."

CHAPTER 79

The closer we got to Halloween, the worse I became. I wouldn't go out except for work, and even then, I didn't want to go there because of the history. Halloween was now only a month away and I felt sick at the thought of it approaching.

Mason was brilliant. He would do online shopping for me, so I didn't see any images relating to Halloween on the retailer's website. Food would then be delivered to the house without having to go to the shops. If we needed anything small, Mason would pick it up for me on his way home from work.

I couldn't sleep, and when I looked at the clock, it was the early hours of the morning. I didn't want to disturb Mason, so I got out of bed. I put the light on in the hall, but it was still dark downstairs. As I was about to make my way down the stairs, I saw a figure at the bottom. My body froze for a moment as I kept staring. I blinked but nothing was there.

Then that creepy voice spoke again. "Are we playing again?"

Through gritted teeth I shouted, "Go away!"

An eerie laugh came in return.

I slowly went down the stairs, keeping my back against the wall. When I got to the bottom, I quickly put the light on so the hallway looked like Blackpool Illuminations. I went into the living room and was about to turn the TV on when a chill brushed down my spine. I quickly turned around, but there was nothing there. I went to turn the lamp on so I could have some light, but a figure was sitting on the sofa. All I remember doing was screaming.

I rushed from the living room. Mason and Mark were already making their way downstairs. They looked at me with concern and each of them asked if I was OK. I was shaking and visibly upset, as I felt like crying.

"There's a figure on the sofa," I said.

They both looked at each other as if I'd gone nuts. They were probably right, but it was the time of year I acted this way. Without getting anything to protect themselves, like I'd expected, they made their way into the living room.

The light went on and Mason said, "Em, come here."

"What have you found? Before I come in there."

"Em, please come here."

As I walked into the living room, Mark was by the sofa.

Mason approached me. "What do you see on the sofa?" he asked.

"A coat."

And then it hit me. I hadn't seen a figure, just a coat.

"Sorry, Em," Mark said. "It's my coat. I just threw it on the sofa, and because it's on top of pillows, I guess in the dark, it looked different."

"Are you trying to give me a heart attack?" I spat back at my brother.

He grabbed the coat. As he walked towards the door, he stopped and turned back towards me. "I am sorry, Em," he repeated, and with that, he quickly disappeared.

Mason looked at me as if I'd lost the plot.

"What?!" I snapped.

"Em, he didn't mean it."

"Do you have any idea what this is like?" I screamed at him. "No, you don't! Anything I see can either be something or nothing. I'm falling apart, or that's how it feels."

Mason didn't say anything to my outburst—and just as well, because I would have been irrational. What he did do was pull me into an embrace.

After my breathing had gone back to normal, I followed Mason upstairs and went back to bed.

When I closed my eyes, all I could see was the mask from *Halloween.* The scene that I'd watched all those years ago as a child replayed in my head. No matter how much I tried, I couldn't think of anything else, so I turned over and cuddled up to Mason in the hopes this would go away.

Mason held my hand in place so I didn't roll to the other side. As I cuddled him, tears streamed down my face, from the terror that I felt, and I let them fall.

CHAPTER 80

The next few weeks sped by and suddenly Halloween was here again. I was dreading nightfall. In the meantime, I pottered around the house, ignoring the fact it was Halloween. For weeks, the voice in my head had been taunting me but I'd tried my best to ignore it. I tried to stay level-headed as much as possible, hoping I wouldn't crack up.

In order to keep busy, I started cleaning the house, trying to ignore what day it was. Although that didn't stop me jumping every time the front door opened or closed, and I always proceeded to the front door with caution until I saw it was either Mason or Mark.

My phone went. When I answered, it was Nancy.

"Hi, Emily—how are you doing?" she asked.

"Terrified, but because I'm in my house, I'm doing OK. What time you in work?"

"I'm just waiting for the train to arrive so I can get to work. I just wanted to know if you're doing OK, and ask when you're back at work?"

"Hopefully in a couple of days. However, as we both know, it depends if they take the decorations down on time before I'm due back!"

"I'll let you know if I hear anything. I better go because I think my train is about to arrive. Speak later."

"Speak later. Bye."

I settled down to watch the TV. I was flicking

through the channels when an advert came up for the film *Scream*. Suddenly, I froze. My stomach churned, making me feel sick, as I fumbled for the remote, unable to look away from the screen in case something happened. When I finally located the remote, I pressed any and all buttons to get the image off the screen.

Once I had changed the channel, the next programme showed a murder scene with someone dressed in a mask. This just wasn't my day. I scrambled once more for the remote to turn over. In the end, I turned the TV off and tried to breathe. I got up and walked away from the living room. My whole body shook as I entered the kitchen.

I placed my hands on the counter, trying to control my breathing as I tried to calm down. I couldn't take much more of this.

I rang the doctors. It must have been an hour later, maybe two, when the doctor finally rang me back. Luckily, it was the same doctor who had spoken to me about the referral to the psychiatrist.

"How can I help, Emily?"

"Well, we both know what day it is, and we know how this affects me. I'm seeing images in my own home because of the TV, and I know there's nothing I can do about that, but the reason I'm ringing… Is there any way to speed up seeing the psychiatrist?"

"You did get the letter from the hospital, right? I have a copy here, and they said that they acknowledge they are going to see you, but there is a waiting list."

"I understand that, but isn't there any way I can get to see them sooner rather than later? I don't know how much more I can take. I'm not sleeping properly, I'm having nightmares and I'm terrified."

"I just looked at your record and I gave you sleeping tablets to help last year. However, I can see that you didn't get sleeping tablets for this year."

"I thought I would try without the sleeping tablets."

"Well, the season will be over by the end of tonight, so I won't give you any sleeping tablets, but for next year, it may be recommended for the week before. How are things with work?"

"Thank you—I'll keep that in mind for next year. As for work, they aren't listening, and I don't know how much more I can take."

"As I said to you before, if you need a sick note for this time of year in the future, then we can do that for you if work are being unreasonable and not allowing you the time off. As for the psychiatrist, I will see if there's anything I can do to speed up the process."

"Thank you."

I don't know what I'd expected, maybe a miracle cure, but I felt simultaneously guilty and relieved that I'd phoned the doctors. I just had this feeling that I'd have to wait a while longer before I got the help I needed.

CHAPTER 81

After Halloween, the months passed quickly, and as usual, I felt myself. Then, out of the blue, a letter from the hospital arrived. They had given me an appointment to outline any treatment they could offer me. The appointment was a month away, so I had a chance to organise time off work so I'd be able to attend.

I have to say, Kim was brilliant. She had no problem with me having time off for this appointment, because we both knew from past experience that I needed the help. I was pleased that I was having the appointment, but also very nervous because I had no idea what these appointments might entail, facing my fear.

Mason was pleased I was going to have these appointments, and he arranged the day off so he could take me. We both knew if someone did not take me, I wouldn't voluntarily go. It wasn't because I didn't want to go, but because of what it was, I needed that push to get there.

As the weeks went by and the appointment got closer, I started to panic and dread filled me at the thought of these sessions. I had an idea of what it might be like, but I wouldn't actually know until I'd spoken to the psychiatrist in the first appointment. I kept thinking of the what-ifs and how I would be affected. My mind was doing overtime thinking through different scenarios, rather than waiting until I was at the hospital.

The day had finally arrived and I was nervous

as I didn't know what to expect. Mason took me to the hospital, but I had to go in the room alone.

A lady came out into the corridor. "Emily Brown?" she said.

I looked up at her and quietly said, "I'm Emily."

"If you would like to follow me, please."

I followed her into a large, plain room with lots of seats inside. She introduced herself and her colleague, who was next to her.

"Hi, I'm one of the psychiatrists here at the hospital. My name is Laura, and this is one of the nurses, David." They must have picked up on my nerves because Laura said, "This is just an initial assessment to find out how we can help you."

"There is nothing to be scared of, because we just want to talk to you and find out what has been going on," David advised.

"OK." I tried to relax, getting ready to answer any questions they had.

The psychiatrist looked at me and started to ask her questions. "You have been referred to us by your doctors as they believe you have a fear of masks, so I would like you to tell us in your own words about this fear?"

I was shaking. I was going to have to talk in detail, all over again, about the masks and Halloween, and I really didn't want to, but I knew I had to so I could get the help.

"I have never liked masks or Halloween, but that was it, I just thought I didn't like it, and so I thought nothing more of it until a few years ago. I remember when I was little, I saw a scene from what I now know to be the film *Halloween*, and I saw a man being sliced up by the man in the mask." I was suddenly aware of how nervous I actually was, being in this hospital and having to explain this in detail. My voice became quieter.

"My dad then bought a helmet—years ago, when I was a child—and poked his tongue out through the mask and this frightened me. But this never interfered with my life until a few years ago. When I started working in a call centre, they decided to put up Halloween decorations. Again, I knew I didn't like it and just tried to get on with my work as best I could. Then on the day of Halloween, I came in to do my job as usual, and I was confronted by people dressed up and wearing masks—about four hundred people—and I completely lost it. I ran into the toilets, terrified, and started panicking, and that was the day I was sent home." I felt as if I'd raced to get all this out without taking a break. It wasn't true, but that's how it felt, because I just wanted this out in the open as quickly as possible so they could start treating me.

"So how is your life now?" David asked.

"Since that day in work, my life has not been the same. I'm more aware of the season and I can't go downtown, because if I see anything in shop windows or inside, I completely go to pieces—I'm terrified. My fiancé, Mason, has to go to the shops for me or I have to order online. All this just to avoid Halloween.

"Having said that, work did a charity event and used masks in the middle of summer last year. I completely freaked out—crying, sweating and I almost became incoherent because I just wanted to get out of there and get to a safe place."

David looked at me, nodded and wrote a few things down.

Then Laura asked, "You say you have a fiancé—are there any problems at home?"

Why were they bringing Mason into this? "No, things are good between us. Apart from when this fear takes hold of me—I must drive him nuts."

They both made more notes.

"Any problems with your sex life?" Laura asked.

What the hell does my sex life have to do with my phobia? "No, there's no issue there."

"Is there any family history of depression, or have you experienced depression?" she asked.

"I went to pieces when I was doing my GCSEs but, as far as I know, there is no family history of depression."

They both wrote more on their pads, and then Laura said to me, "Thank you for coming today. And I'm sorry we've had to ask a lot of these questions, but I do think we might be able to help you. This would mean controlled exposure to masks, in particular the horror genre. This will then, hopefully, help you to cope with your fear of masks."

I was curious, so I had to ask, "I have been told that this is probably a phobia—would that be right?"

"It does sound very much like a phobia, and this is why we are going to attempt a controlled exposure to masks. I don't know the name of the phobia off-hand, but yes, you definitely have a phobia."

I arranged my next appointment with them to do this controlled exposure, and when I left, I had mixed feelings. I wanted the help, I knew I needed the help, but the thought of going into that room to be exposed to the one thing I hated the most terrified me. It would take all of my energy and willpower to go to these appointments.

CHAPTER 82

I made arrangements to have the following Friday off work and my appointment was set for ten o'clock in the morning. When Friday finally came and the alarm went off, I had no problem getting up. I carried on with things around the house as if nothing was going on.

Mason came downstairs. "Are you ready for your appointment?" he said.

My stomach was tying in little knots at the thought. I was shaking and I felt sick. "I'm ready."

He ran his hand down my arm and smiled warmly. "It's going to be alright, and I'll be outside if you need me."

I smiled back as I got my jacket. "Let's get going. The sooner I get there, the sooner I get home."

* * *

While I waited in the corridor, all I could think was, *Run. That way you don't have to face anything.* As I contemplated this, the door opened, and the man who had been in the initial assessment meeting was standing there.

"Emily, if you would like to come in."

I followed him into this small office, which was not what I was expecting, and sat down by the desk. I don't know what I'd imagined the room would be like—not this, certainly—but still, I was here and dreading every moment of it.

"Let me introduce myself again, in case you've forgotten," said the man. He was tall, slim and smartly dressed, and his black hair matched his tidy appearance. "My name is David and I am one of the nurses in this department."

"I thought I was going to be seeing a psychiatrist, like the lady I saw last week with you?"

"After you left there was a discussion and, considering the circumstances because we had declined to help you in the past, we felt that I have enough experience to be able to help you with your controlled exposure to masks."

"Oh, I see. As long as I get help, I'm fine with this."

I could have chatted in the office all day as long as I avoided any masks. However, David was there to try and help me, so avoiding the inevitable wouldn't last much longer.

"Just so you can relax—you won't be exposed to any masks today."

Relief flooded through me and my body relaxed. The tension was gone.

David continued, "The sessions will last approximately an hour each week, but today I am going to try and determine what masks you are afraid of and then discuss this with you, so we'll have something to work with for our next session."

"I see. How long will the sessions last? Is there a time limit?"

He put his pen down and looked me straight in the eye. "There is no time limit as such. All this will depend on how you react and what you want out of this."

I sat back in the chair, trying to make myself comfortable. "I just want to get better. I want this all to be over and have my life back...you know, normality."

"Now, you say that you are afraid of masks,

especially those from the horror genre, but are you afraid of any other masks?"

I thought about my answer for a few moments, because I had the feeling that a simple no would not be enough.

"I'm not afraid of any other masks—for example, a surgical mask or masks from Mardi Gras—but I wouldn't wear one."

"OK. Anything else?"

"Yes, actually there is. I just remembered, I don't like the smell of plastic because it reminds me of masks. I know it doesn't make any sense, but that's something else."

He wrote a few notes down and then asked, "You mentioned surgical and Mardi Gras masks and that you're OK with them. Can you explain in a bit more detail about that?"

I felt like this was really twenty questions, but I understood the reasoning behind it.

"Seeing a surgical mask or Mardi Gras masks, on TV or in person, I'm not frightened of them. I remember once, my mum having masks up on the wall as you went up the stairs, and they were very pretty." I couldn't believe I'd forgotten about that until just that moment. "I remember my mum asking for my permission so she could put them on the wall. Anyway, I thought they were pretty because they were nicely decorated, so I never had a problem with them."

"You say you won't wear a mask—is that just the horror mask or any of them?"

I thought for a moment and then recalled an incident in work. "I remember being in work, and a woman was really ill; the ambulance was called. Anyway, when they got there, they were treating her and put an oxygen mask on her so that she could breathe. The thought of a mask—even an oxygen mask—on me...it won't happen, ever."

He looked at me as he digested the information. "Have you ever had an oxygen mask on you?"

"I had a knee operation a couple years ago and I remember coming around and this mask was over my face, so I pulled it off and threw it on the floor. The nurse was not impressed, but I didn't care. I don't like anything on my face. That probably comes from a time when I was given a plastic nose so I could wear it as part of a witch's costume. I remember it smelled terrible—like the plastic I was telling you about earlier. My mum even tried to put talcum powder in it to make it smell better for me, but I couldn't stand it. So I pulled it off as hard as I could to break the elastic on the nose so I couldn't be made to wear it again."

David nodded and made a few more notes before checking his watch. "Well, we've almost completed the hour and you have given me a lot of information. It looks like you're remembering a lot more information as you are talking about it, which is good. So, this gives me a few ideas on how we can proceed for the next session."

We arranged the same time the following Friday. As I left, I felt alright, for the first time in a long time. I'd remembered things, things that might help me in the long term, and it felt great.

CHAPTER 83

I didn't talk much as we drove home. I opened the front door, made my way to the kitchen and put the kettle on.

"Are you going to tell me what happened in the session today?" Mason said.

I turned to him. "I just spoke at length about my phobia and, as we got chatting, I remembered more things. Things that I thought weren't relevant until we discussed it."

"Like…?" he asked impatiently.

"Like… I don't like having anything on my face—for example, an oxygen mask."

He looked at me strangely. "You never told me that."

I sighed and rolled my eyes. "I told you when we first met that I'd had an operation on my knee. I know it was a long time ago, but I just remember waking up and this mask was on me and I just took it off. To be honest, I didn't think much of it until today, but apparently it has relevance."

Mason finished off making the drinks as I sat down. He handed my drink to me and we discussed in more detail how my session went.

* * *

When I went into work, I was cornered by Kim.

"How did the session go on Friday?" she asked.

I was taken aback by the fact that she'd even remembered I had an appointment.

"It was the first appointment and we discussed a lot. I was starting to remember things that I completely had forgotten about, and I have another one on Friday."

"Well, that is good news, and hopefully they'll be able to help you." Kim beamed a smile at me. Of course, she was relieved—she thought the workplace would be off the hook for everything that had happened in the meantime.

* * *

The next session came around really quickly. It was the same routine—I panicked, and Mason drove me to make sure I actually went to the session, rather than pretend I did.

When I was in the room with David again, we went through a few more things and then he pulled out some items—a surgical mask and a few animal masks—and laid them on the table. *Nothing like getting straight into this*, I thought.

"So, as you can see, I have brought with me today some different types of masks. What I want to know from you is how you feel about them?"

I looked at them in turn, and then I replied, "I'm OK with them."

However, he looked as if he didn't believe me. It could have been my reaction, but he asked, "Are you sure about that?"

I looked at them again, carefully. I could feel my body react to them. It wasn't like my reaction to the horror masks, but there was a dislike of them.

"As I said last week, I'm fine with the surgical mask, but it's these other masks that make me uncomfortable. Not like the horror type, but I just don't like them."

David jotted a few things down on his pad. He tapped his pen from side to side as he thought for a moment.

"Right, we will start simple. I want you to pick up the surgical mask first."

I looked over to the table and I picked up the surgical mask. "As I said, I have no problem with a surgical mask."

He leaned over to his right, opened the desk drawer and pulled out another surgical mask. "I am going to put this surgical mask on because I want to see your reaction. Then I want you to put it on as well."

I watched as he put on the surgical mask.

"How does this make you feel?" he asked.

"I'm OK. As I said, this type of mask I don't have problems with. Probably because it's something good."

Still wearing the mask, he replied, "Yes, your response to this is different because you associate it with a good thing rather than a bad thing. Now, like I said earlier, I want you to put one on as well."

I put the surgical mask on. I felt fine and I told him this. He seemed pleased at this reaction and then asked that I remove the surgical mask and give it back to him. I did, and then he continued.

"You stated earlier that you dislike the masks in front of you, but after finding out you're OK with the surgical mask, I believe your dislike is of these animal masks. Is this correct?"

I looked at them again before saying, "Yes, I feel very uneasy around them."

"Can you explain in more detail to me, please?"

"It isn't that they're animal-decorated—I think it's to do with the fact that there are no eyes and no real mouth. However, I think it is more to do with the eyes because they've been cut out. I remember as a child I had an Aunt Sally mask—from the show *Worzel Gummidge*. I loved the show, but this mask, it was so creepy. I disliked it that much that I hid it under a chair and put things on top of it."

"And you never wore this mask?"

"Never. I was just glad my mum finally got rid of it."

David wrote a few more things on his pad. "Would you be willing to try one on, or even touch one?"

These masks were not terrifying, but I felt uncomfortable around them. However, I wanted the help, so I agreed to try. The three animal masks were a cow, a frog and a dog, each with the eyes cut out. My whole body trembled as I picked each one up in turn to look at them, explaining each time how uncomfortable I felt.

After a few minutes of picking up and holding these masks, I started to feel better, but when I tried to put one to my face, I couldn't do it. The smell of plastic made my stomach churn, and suddenly I felt sick.

David noticed my reaction. "I'm going to give you some homework," he said. "I want you to take these masks home with you and play around with them so you become more familiar and relaxed around them. Are you OK with this?"

"I'll give it a go, but I can't promise anything."

He put them in a bag for me, and we made a follow-up appointment for next Friday.

CHAPTER 84

Over the next week, I took the masks out of the bag and laid them on the table. I did what David had suggested; I picked them up, held them, but each time I tried to put them near my face, I just could not do it.

After I'd been doing this for a few days, Mason asked, "How are you doing?"

I sighed. "I could be doing better, but I just can't bring it to my face. I've tried."

"If you've tried and you can't, don't beat yourself up over it."

Mason even went as far as putting on one of the animal masks in front of me. He looked weird, but I felt OK. I could feel myself reacting, but I wasn't terrified. I didn't want to run from the room and hide and, after a few minutes, I felt calm. He took the mask off and gave it back to me, rather than putting it on the table. For a moment, I held it, and then tried to put it near my face again, as if I was going to put it on. However, the smell continued to churn my stomach, and I just couldn't do it.

I came to the conclusion that I was just going to have to tell David that it wasn't possible for me to wear even this type of mask, although I could at least pick it up and hold it in my hands.

When I had the next session, David was pleased with my progress so far, even though I couldn't put the mask on. He went on to show me images. They were of a variety of different types of masks, all from different places and contexts, from the surgical mask to the horror mask. There were even images of a burqa.

"Does this hold any reaction for you?" David asked when he showed me it.

I was shocked. "No—I'm fine with people wearing this."

I was even fine when he showed me a clown mask. However, when I was shown a horror image, I felt very uncomfortable and he saw this in me. We must have gone through about twenty or thirty images, but luckily there were not many horror images.

"Describe what you are feeling as you are seeing this image," he said, referring to the horror image.

"My mouth feels dry and I can feel my body starting to shake, and I'm feeling very uncomfortable."

He nodded as he considered that for a moment, and then wrote something down on his pad again.

"As part of the treatment, we had to check that you had no other issues with any type of mask, whether that be religious or fantasy. However, we can see that you definitely have more of an issue with horror masks, so I will work on this. Having said that, you did have an issue with simple animal masks. Even though you can't wear them, at least you are now able to hold one and look at it without any reaction—that would have caused significant discomfort to you all your life."

"OK."

"I'm going to be honest with you. With this controlled exposure programme, next week, I am going to bring in a few horror masks and gauge your reaction."

My stomach was turning into knots at the thought of having to come here next week with those masks in the room, but I tried to stay as calm as I could.

"We are doing this so soon?"

He looked at me with puzzlement. "That is what you're here for. I know it will be daunting for you, but this is part of the programme, and so far, you are doing really well."

I agreed with him—so far, I *had* done really well—but the thought of coming next week made me want to run and hide and pretend this was not going to happen. However, the other side of me wanted to get this over and done with in the hopes that somehow, I could cope with Halloween and this season. I wanted to be able to go downtown and look in shop windows and not freak out. I wanted to be able to go to the shops, go inside, do what I needed to do and come back out again without being terrified and scared of what might happen to me.

I reluctantly made the appointment for the following Friday and left the hospital, shaking.

CHAPTER 85

When I got home, I put the envelope of images on the table. A while later, when I was upstairs in the bedroom, Mason called up.

"That envelope hasn't moved yet."

I knew he was pointing out the obvious, but I didn't want to open that envelope again.

"I'll look at it when I'm ready," I shouted back at him.

Suddenly, he was standing in the doorway. "The whole point of these sessions is to get you to face your fear and not to hide from it."

"What would you know?" I glared at him as he stood there. "I will do this in my own time, and not when you—or anybody—tells me to."

"Suit yourself." He turned around and went back downstairs.

I finished putting the clothes away and headed to the kitchen. On the table, the envelope was still waiting for me. I stared at it as I put the kettle on. Once I'd made my drink, I sat at the table and continued to look at the envelope.

Mason was right, I needed to do this. I opened the envelope and pulled out the images. I looked at each one when in turn, carefully, and felt fine. As of yet, I hadn't come across any horror images, but with each image I was fine with, I got closer to the last few images—the horror ones.

When I turned over the next image, it was from a horror film, I knew that instantly. Suddenly, my head was spinning, my mouth was dry and I didn't like it. I quickly turned the image over and backed away. I just kept staring at the table, where the image lay face down, and felt my stomach churn.

I was about to leave the kitchen when Mason walked in.

"I see you opened the envelope?"

"I did, but I was just leaving," I snapped.

He looked shocked, and as I went to walk past him, he grabbed my arm. "Em, you have to do this, and you can't leave them lying on the table."

I pulled my arm away from him. "And why not?" I asked bluntly.

He tilted his head towards me sympathetically. "You know why. You have to do what they've asked of you—this is the only way you can move forward."

"Maybe I've changed my mind. Maybe I don't want to move forward. Maybe I want to stay like this forever."

"Now you're being ridiculous. Why don't you just sit at the table, take a deep breath, and try again?"

The thought of facing the image again made me panic. "I don't want to try again. I've had enough for one day and, to be honest, the thought of these images in my house... I just don't like it."

He pulled me in for a hug. "I know you don't," he said sweetly, "but if you want to get better, this is what you have to do."

"It's just the nightmares will start up again, and this is stressing me out. I just don't know if I can do this. I'm terrified—and any other horrible word you can think of that describes this."

"You have to do this," he said, holding my gaze.

"I know—why don't you do this, and then I can go back and say I did it," I said with sarcasm.

He smiled softly at me. "Nice try, but we both

know you're the one who has to do this. Now sit at the table, take a deep breath and try again."

I trembled at the thought of voluntarily looking at these horror images again, but I had no choice.

I sat back down at the table, pulled the chair in closer, and turned the image back around.

CHAPTER 86

When I went back for my next session the following week, I was confronted with horror masks. David had warned me that this was going to happen, but I didn't believe it until I was actually there.

He pulled each mask out of the bag in turn and asked me to look at it. My body went tense, I felt sick and all I could do was retch—nothing came out. I watched as David played about with the masks and listened to what he described.

"As you can see, this is a Scream mask. The mask is made from simple material—it's light so the person can wear it—but nothing is going to happen. Now, what I want you to do is to hold this mask."

I shook my head in defiance—that wasn't going to happen any time soon. Hell, I wanted to bolt right out of the room. The only reason I stayed was because I'd asked for the help. I was prepared to take baby steps, but this felt too much.

I kept staring at the mask. If I took my eyes off it, something would happen to me. I was shaking and panic built inside me as I kept my eye on this mask.

"I can't do it."

"OK. Can you describe to me why you cannot?"

I pulled away from the desk as much as I could in that small room and started to describe my feelings. Once I'd told him, he asked if I wanted to go to the bathroom. It was so tempting to go and that way I wouldn't have had to come back, but I was there for a reason. To my surprise, I declined the offer.

"I want to run. In fact, I want to bolt through that door and never come back."

He nodded that he understood. "This is what's known as the flight response, and it doesn't surprise me. I can see by your reaction that you are very uncomfortable around this mask." He put the mask away for a moment while we spoke.

"When I first attended these sessions," I said, "I felt fine coming here, but now it's taking all of my willpower just to get here."

"Then can I ask how you get here, if this is the way you feel?"

"My fiancé has rearranged his work schedule so he has the day off. This is so he can bring me to the sessions, to make sure I get here and attend."

He smiled at me. "So you've created a backup plan, as it were, to get here because you do not trust yourself."

"That sounds about right. I don't trust myself to come here to the sessions without help."

"You're not the first person that has done this. You, the patient, know you need help, but to make sure you get here, you've created a scenario to make sure that you do. Now, let's get this mask out again and see if you can deal with it. Is that alright?"

"Not really, but I will give it a go."

He showed me the mask again, and my body reacted harshly. The more I was exposed to this mask, the worse my symptoms became.

David pulled out a different horror mask, and my reaction was the same—panic, anxiety, dry mouth, the list went on. I just kept getting bombarded with different masks, and I hated it.

When he finally put the last mask away, David asked, "How are you feeling?"

How the hell do you think I'm feeling? I'm feeling like shit, I wanted to scream. Instead, I fidgeted in my seat. By now, I felt very uncomfortable being in this room. As calmly as possible, I replied, "I have just had enough for today and I want to go home."

He nodded in agreement. "I understand, and I agree. However, as you can see, the masks are in this bag. I want you to take them home and get them out and look at them and try and play about with them."

Had he just said what I thought he said? I must've had a look of sheer horror on my face when he added, "I am being serious. Try and do this."

"I don't think I can do that. I'm panicking at the thought of even holding the bag." My nerves were evident in my voice and body language.

"Emily, you need to try. I'll put this into a bigger bag for you, but let's see how you go."

CHAPTER 87

I felt sick to my stomach knowing that the masks were in the house. I left them hooked over the radiator in the hall and tried to forget they were there. Mason tried to bring the bag into the living room and I completely freaked out.

"Get that bag out of here now!"

"Em, you have to do—"

I interrupted him. "No, I do not, and I would appreciate it if you didn't try and put pressure on me!"

Mason, still holding the bag, put it back where he'd found it and left the subject alone.

* * *

With each session at the hospital, I was getting worse. My stress levels were through the roof, my symptoms of panic and anxiety were even more present, and the thought of going back for each session absolutely terrified me. Each week, the sessions became harder, and although David was a lovely person, I just didn't want to be there anymore. The sessions weren't making any difference, and that upset me.

My penultimate session stayed with me. I went in as usual, thanks to Mason getting me there in the first place. I sat in the room and David asked general questions.

"Are you ready to get started?" he added.

"I guess so."

He loaded up the computer, and while he waited for it to come to life, he said, "What we are going to do today is look at some images on the computer screen. I know that since we had masks in the room, you may think this is taking a step backwards, but I want to see how you react to these images on the screen, as this is something we have discussed in the sessions. I know this might be tough for you, but I want you to do the best you can, alright?"

I nodded in agreement but didn't say anything as I waited for him to turn on the screen. I thought I was going to see an image straightaway, but I didn't—it was just a screensaver that appeared. I felt as if I could breathe at that point, but then he said words I dreaded.

"Right—I'm going to open the first picture."

He clicked on the first image. It was a horror mask. I don't know what it was from—it was nothing I'd seen before or knew about, which was fine by me, not that I needed to know anything about it to feel terrified.

It was the same with each image. I felt sick, my body was shaking, fear swept through me in hot and cold flushes. I wanted to cry to relieve the terror and panic.

Then came an image I'd never forget, no matter how much I tried. From that day forth, it would be with me forever.

It was a woman dressed in white, with long dark hair, a pale complexion and an expression I could only describe as making me want to run for my life. I think she was dressed as a vampire, but it was the most terrifying one I'd ever seen. There was no soul in the eyes, the teeth were yellow and her face was covered in blood. My body reacted so badly—tears streamed down my face, and my whole body shook like nothing I'd experienced before or since.

As David kept the image on the screen, he even admitted that he didn't like this one. He told me where it was from, but luckily I didn't remember, or I chose to forget—either way, I'm grateful for that blockage in my memory.

When he turned off the image, David turned back at me. "How are you feeling?"

"Terrified, I'm shaking and I feel so sick." I rocked back and forth as if I had regressed to a child.

"I will admit that if I saw that image for real on the streets, even I would run."

I tried to wipe the tears away, but that didn't stop them coming. "It's nice to hear that I'm not the only one. I'd never seen anything like that before. Where did you get it?" I don't know why I asked that, but I did.

"With the help of my colleague, I looked for images on the internet and this was one of the ones we found."

I was still rocking back and forth, trying to calm myself down, when he finally said, "I think we can call it a day."

I'd never left the office so fast.

CHAPTER 88

I ran over to the car and Mason opened the door.

"Are you OK?"

I couldn't say anything as I was trying to throw up in the gutter, next to the car. When my stomach had settled a little, I replied, still shaking, "This was the worst session I've ever been to. I was just bombarded with horror image after horror image, and then I saw this image and now I'll never get it out of my head."

Mason took me home, made me a drink and said, "I'm going to clean my car, but I'll be right outside if you need me."

I knew I was safe, but the panic and the fear was still ever so present and I started freaking out. I quickly opened the door and went over to the car.

"You don't like cleaning cars, so why are you here?" he asked.

"I just want company, that's all."

Mason didn't respond, because I think he knew why I'd come outside. After he'd finished cleaning the car, we went back inside.

"Let me take you out for food," he said. "Pub lunch?"

I smiled weakly but replied, "That sounds nice. I'll get my jacket."

When we got to the pub, Mason went to the bar and got a few drinks while I looked at the menu. I was still shaking and I was very aware of my surroundings. I watched everyone around me, in case something was going to happen. Suddenly, I needed the bathroom, but I didn't want to go because I didn't want to leave Mason's side.

"Em, you do have to go to the bathroom. You will be fine, I promise."

I didn't answer as I left the table. I looked up at the long, winding stairs to the women's bathroom. I hesitated at first, but I really needed to go, so I made my way up the stairs.

When I entered the bathroom, it was huge. There were many places where somebody could have hidden and terrified me, so I quickly looked around before using one of the cubicles. All my senses were more alert than they'd ever been and I was so afraid. I'd never used a bathroom so quickly just to get out of there.

I ran downstairs and quickly walked back to the table.

Mason and I spent a few hours at the pub, but it didn't help settle my nerves. The images I'd been bombarded with were still very much in my mind. I felt sorry for Mason, because for the rest of the day, I was his shadow. When we were home, if he went upstairs, I went with him. If he went to the kitchen, I went with him. This played out for the next twenty-four hours until I had completely calmed down.

Due to the sessions getting harder each week, it didn't surprise me that this session had affected me really badly. When I was back to normal and thought about it, it made sense that due to the intense nature of that session, I'd reacted so badly and it had taken me so long to come back around.

* * *

Another Friday rolled around and I was absolutely terrified to go into the session—after the previous week, I wasn't surprised, and neither was David.

He looked at me as he relaxed back in his chair. "How were you after you left the office last week?"

"I went up to the car and started retching because my body wanted me to be sick. I became my fiancé's shadow, and that was ridiculous."

"Looking back on it, you might think it was ridiculous to be his shadow but you probably needed it."

"He took me to the pub, but that didn't work. All my senses were on high alert and I suspected everybody in that pub. Even though nothing happened. That image you showed me—it's now embedded in my head and it will always be there."

He wrote on his pad, and then looked at me. "Yes, it's not an image that would leave anyone anytime soon, including myself. I have been discussing your sessions with the psychiatrist, the woman you saw in the first session, about how you were making progress initially. However, over the last few weeks, the sessions have become what we would call counterproductive. This is why, after many months of trying to help, I don't think we can help any further. The only other help we could possibly recommend is what we call flooding."

I looked puzzled and had to ask, "What is flooding?"

"Flooding is when we would put you in a room with masks and images that would completely surround you. This would mean you would be in that room until your symptoms, such as panic, had subsided."

"I don't think I'm ready for that."

He smiled and replied, "I can understand why you wouldn't be ready right now. Over the last few months, you have been through quite a bit, and I think last week really took a toll on you. However, maybe you could consider it in the future."

"I will think about it, but not right now. I need to let myself calm down," I said hesitantly.

"I will write to your doctor to let him know what's happened in the sessions, and he will contact you if necessary."

Knowing that this was going to be my last session, I breathed a sigh of relief.

"Thank you, David, for at least trying to help me, but I think I'm stuck with this."

"Well, don't sell yourself short. You did make progress. Through our discussions, you remembered you couldn't hold any masks—for example, the animal ones—but you did, and you tried to put one on. So even though you haven't overcome the horror masks, you have made progress, even if you don't think so."

CHAPTER 89

At work, I had to attend another meeting, this time with HR because of all the time I had taken off over the phobia. They wanted to see if they could help further. I had just finished my sessions at the hospital and I really didn't want to go and talk about this all over again. However, despite my nerves, Michael and I were ready for the meeting.

I'd seen the woman holding the meeting in passing, but we had never spoken. She introduced herself as Tracey.

"How are you feeling?" she asked.

Due to the fact Halloween was only around the corner, I wasn't at my best. "Nervous about being here, as I don't feel safe."

"This is why we brought the meeting down here, so you would feel comfortable."

I nodded that I was OK with the room. As the meeting continued, I had to admit what the sessions had put me through and how ill I had become.

It took all my strength not to walk out. I just could not bring myself to continue. The sessions for my phobia had taken their toll.

Tracey asked the same questions that pretty much all of management had asked in the meetings and the grievance meetings. I told her that I had to take time off for this period using holiday days. I then had to explain to her that the hospital had advised that this phobia was too embedded for me to get help.

The meeting seemed to go on forever and I really wanted to leave. After the counselling sessions, I felt worn down and unable to focus properly, and I didn't want to talk about it anymore, but Tracey kept going on and on. Then she said something that really shocked me.

"I have to ask: can't you just get over this?"

Had she really just asked the stupidest question I could think of? I stayed silent for a moment before replying, "We have been talking in this meeting and I have told you that this is a phobia. This is not a dislike and not something that can be fixed easily. So, in answer to your question, no, I cannot just get over it."

I think she realised what she had said had affected me. "I didn't mean it like that. What I was trying to get at was: would you be able to get over it with help?"

"I thought the sessions would help me, but as I said earlier, they think it's too embedded for me to get the help I need. So it looks like I'm stuck with this phobia."

I'd had that many meetings on this subject, I knew each meeting would just go around in circles. Nothing was going to change, as they were never going to admit the part they had played in this.

So, after a long meeting, we signed the papers, and I quickly left the building.

CHAPTER 90

In a few weeks' time, it was going to be Halloween all over again. I'd hoped that the sessions at the hospital would have helped me with this phobia, but I felt as if I was back to square one, with no hope of getting better.

The voice in my head kept taunting me. "I tried to tell you. It was never going to work, so you're stuck with me."

I started to cry—I was never going to get better.

I made an appointment with the doctor to discuss what had happened in the sessions. A few days later, when I spoke to him, he asked how I felt about the sessions and whether they had helped.

"I'm still scared of horror masks," I said, "and I'm stuck with it."

"I received the letter from the hospital, and even though they felt the sessions were becoming counterproductive, they did say that they could confirm without a doubt that you have the condition they call Samhainophobia, which—as you know—is a fear of Halloween, particularly of horror masks. The other condition is Maskaphobia, which, as they have stated, you have to some degree as it refers to masks in general."

I wanted to start crying again. I felt trapped in this never-ending loop.

"Is there anything I can do to get better and over this phobia?"

The look on the doctor's face said it all. "Unfortunately not. I would have recommended hypnosis, because that can sometimes work, but with what has been said in the letter and the fact that they stated the sessions were counterproductive towards the end, I recommend that you do not go to hypnosis. This is because if there's anything else that you might not be aware of in your background, then hypnosis could open other things that could be more harmful to you."

With that, the last of my hopes were dashed.

"I understand. I guess I just have to manage it the best way I know how," I said. "There was another thing when I was in the sessions—please can you put on my medical record that I don't like oxygen masks on me, as you never know when that's going be needed. It's just so you can warn them in advance."

He gave me a smile and politely said, "Don't worry—I'll put that on your record, and I'll also state that you have this phobia."

"Thank you."

I left the surgery and made my way home. I kept my head down, looking at the floor in case I saw anything in house windows. When I got home, I found a letter from the hospital, addressed to me. The doctor had told me that they were sending me a copy, so I opened it.

The hospital had stated that I had acute symptoms of panic and anxiety that were associated with coming into contact with masks, particularly Halloween masks. They went on to say what my phobia was called, and it was exactly what the doctor had told me. The part I found interesting was that they stated it was particularly disabling for me as it led to extreme anxiety, panic and often acute fear of being attacked. They said in the letter that my symptoms could last from a few hours up to a few days, if not weeks, following exposure. This was not news to me, but this letter was being sent to my workplace and I would take my copy in to show them. I hoped they would take what it said seriously.

What I found really nice was that the hospital acknowledged that work would have to be sensitive and respectful due to this condition. After reading this letter, I had a feeling that work would brush it aside and not take on board what the hospital had advised.

I took a copy of the letter into work and, when I showed it to Kim, she was nice about it, but after a consultation with HR, she gave me the news that the company could not guarantee that there would be no masks in the building and that there was nothing they could do, other than allow me to have the time off over Halloween.

I wasn't surprised. Even when the union had tried to see if there was anything else they could do for me, they'd found that there was no legal ground for a case, probably due to the fact that my condition was so different.

That being said, there were some good team leaders at work. Once I had finished my sessions and meetings in work, all team leaders and upper management knew my name and were aware of my phobia. I'd like to say that that was a good thing, but on the other hand, I didn't want everyone to be so aware of me. One manager even approached me and knew me by name when I'd never even met them.

The good team leaders—or that's what I called them—showed me not only understanding but empathy. In one incident, I had to go in on my day off to get something. The team leader noticed me and said, "Emily, how about you go the other way around." When I looked puzzled, then he added, "There are masks on the other side—nobody expected you in because it was your day off."

I didn't need to be told twice and I went the other way, which meant I avoided a panic attack.

The following day, after I had checked the building was clear, I went over to that team leader and thanked him. It was clear by what he'd done the previous day and the conversation we had that he'd thought about my welfare and considered the impact this would have. I would always be grateful for that.

* * *

I'd wanted so badly for that burden to lift, for my nightmare to be over. I'd wanted a choice; I wanted to be able to go out to the shops when they put the decorations up and be OK. I would have liked to be able to go to work and be fine if they put masks up or Halloween decorations. All I ever wanted was to be able to tolerate Halloween so I wouldn't get scared. If somebody knocked the door trick-or-treating, I wanted to answer it and be fine giving them sweets, but I'd never be able to do that now.

This phobia changed my life. When September comes, I know it won't be long before the shops advertise for Halloween and that means I can't go downtown. I can't go out in case I see anything. I lock myself away and never answer the door to the outside world, just so I can avoid my fear.

I had always hoped I could overcome this phobia as I had put myself through hell and back trying, but the truth is that I'm stuck with this for the rest of my life.

I was asked once, "Can't you just get over it?"

My response would be, now, "I wish I could, but I can't."

AUTHOR PROFILE

I wrote as a hobby for many years, but suddenly, I lost my way. So I decided to take up a free course at The Open University. I loved the course, so I started a degree in English and Creative Writing. I'm currently in my second year.

I started to write this book in the hopes that I would find it therapeutic as I battle with the same phobia as in the book. However, the emotions that resurfaced were painful at times and sometimes overwhelming, but it pushed me to continue writing and finish the book.

<u>Publisher Information</u>

Rowanvale Books provides publishing services to independent authors, writers and poets all over the globe. We deliver a personal, honest and efficient service that allows authors to see their work published, while remaining in control of the process and retaining their creativity. By making publishing services available to authors in a cost-effective and ethical way, we at Rowanvale Books hope to ensure that the local, national and international community benefits from a steady stream of good quality literature.

For more information about us, our authors or our publications, please get in touch.

www.rowanvalebooks.com
info@rowanvalebooks.com

www.ingramcontent.com/pod-product-compliance
Lightning Source LLC
Chambersburg PA
CBHW022139170626
46807CB00005B/2004